T0078125

Clara

FROM TRIALS TO TRIUMPH

LOIS HETTINGER

WESTBOW
PRESS®
A DIVISION OF THOMAS NELSON
& ZONDERVAN

WestBow Press books may be ordered through booksellers or by contacting:

WestBow Press
A Division of Thomas Nelson & Zondervan
1663 Liberty Drive
Bloomington, IN 47403
www.westbowpress.com
1 (866) 928-1240

ISBN: 978-1-9736-0369-6 (sc)
ISBN: 978-1-9736-0368-9 (hc)
ISBN: 978-1-9736-0370-2 (e)

Library of Congress Control Number: 2017915275

Print information available on the last page.

WestBow Press rev. date: 10/24/2017

Chapter 1

W HAT A GLORIOUS MORNING it had been! The birds were singing, the sky was a brilliant blue, and smells of late spring were all around. The trees were heavy with new leaves. In early fall they had looked old, but now they were fresh and vibrant. The warm sun soothed and healed many aches and pains Inez felt, but now, as she stood and looked up, there was a small cloud in the sky. Standing there for a moment to rest from her planting, she surveyed the farm in Middleville, Michigan. It was built on the hillside and very rocky, but the price Inez and her husband, Israel, had paid for the farm was manageable and the house livable. Everywhere Inez looked, there was work to be done, but they were young, and they could do it. They felt privileged to own a farm at such young ages.

As Inez stood looking up, she noticed the cloud seemed to be growing larger and coming closer. Before long, the sun was lost and rain was threatening. She had hoped the rain would hold off until her garden was completely in, but the new life within her was growing and she was moving more slowly these days. At the top of the hill, Israel was clearing stones to plant the first crop of corn in the upper field. He would soon be coming down for lunch.

At the end of the row, Inez looked up to see that the cloud had moved in. She hurried to the house just in time to avoid large drops of rain.

Inez entered the kitchen through the shed. Taking a pan from the cupboard, she opened the last pint of soup brought up from the cellar the previous night. Then she sliced a fresh loaf of the bread she had baked that morning. The cream pie left over from supper would do nicely for dessert, she thought.

Inez glanced out of kitchen window just in time to see Israel coming through the yard gate. Her heart skipped a beat as she looked at this handsome man she was blessed to call her husband. Israel's dark hair and olive complexion always gave her a little thrill. She loved his strong cheekbones and was so proud and content with him.

As Inez finished setting the table for lunch, she felt a little pain in the bottom of her stomach. With two more months before the baby was due, she was puzzled by the pain.

Israel walked through the door just in time to catch the expression of pain and surprise on her face. "Are you all right, Inez?" he asked, looking at her with concern.

"Yes. Just a little pain from the position I was in all morning planting the garden. I suppose it cramped the baby a little."

After lunch, the rain was falling in sheets, delaying the work they both needed to do outside. Well, the work would have to wait until the rain stopped. The soup was refreshing, and the copper teakettle glowed on the cook stove as Inez lit the kerosene lamps. Tomcat sat on the sideboard with his motor running and his tail swishing; he liked the company. Israel walked over to his easel, picked up the pallet, wet the paints, and started making strokes on the fresh canvas he had prepared by painting over a picture last night after they returned from a walk. This would be a still life of the spring wildflowers Inez and he had gathered.

The walk had been so refreshing, with the bright-colored grass of spring along the path of the creek and the swollen stream dancing swiftly by. They had talked of their plans for the future and felt like the world and all its beauty was theirs. The trees were all dressed in new green leaves, and flowers dotted the hillside, beckoning them to come and pick a basketful to bring home.

Now Israel was working on capturing their loveliness. Painting was his first love, but farming was a necessity if he was to make a living for the family they were counting on. Inez went to the prized treadle sewing machine her parents had given her for a wedding present to work on some of the last of the baby clothes. She sewed each little tuck with care for the baby she was carrying beneath her heart. Since she could remember, she had dreamed of having children. Now, in just two short months, it would be a reality. Inez's sister, soon-to-be Aunt Genie, thought she was fussing way too much and should make more practical dresses, but Inez couldn't help adding the sweet little tucks and lace. Her first baby! She could hardly believe it! She felt the child within her and knew it was the girl she had dreamed of, but she was afraid to tell a soul in case she was wrong. Then, too, she knew Israel wanted a boy to help him build the farm and to inherit it someday.

As Inez stood up, she felt a pain sharper than the earlier one.

A look of concern crossed Israel's face as he glanced at her. "Are you all right?" he asked again. "It's not time for the baby, is it?"

"It can't be. I still have two months to go," she replied with a worried look.

As the afternoon wore on, however, the pain became more intense. Inez finished the dress she was working on and stood up to prepare supper just as another contraction hit, doubling her over. "Time for the baby or not, I think it's on the way," she said.

That was all Israel needed. "I'll go up the hill and get Mrs. Snow, and then I'll go get Dr. Simons," he said as he crossed the kitchen and pulled his windbreaker from the closet behind the stove.

Inez sat down in the rocker by the stove to wait. Silently she prayed.

> *Dear God, I know you love this baby even more than I do. Please take care of it. It's not time yet, but it seems it's anxious to make an entrance into the world. Keep it safe, I pray. I've waited so long for her. I promise to love her and train her as you would have me. Please, Lord, if it be thy will, give us a safe delivery.*

As she waited, she thought about her own childhood.

Inez had been raised in a large family. She felt the love and discipline of her stern mother and adventurous father, who had come to America from Denmark on a ship. The crossing turned out to be treacherous, but he'd finally made it and eventually settled in Michigan, where he met his wife, Martha. At that time, Martha already had seven children and had lost her husband. Martha and Peter were married and raised four more children, including Inez. The children were raised to love God and each other, and Peter taught them to love and value life. Martha taught the children that home was a sanctuary and to worship the Creator and to keep home free of unnecessary dirt and clutter at all times. She raised her children with these values and still gave them love and freedom to be themselves.

Mrs. Snow came through the kitchen door and interrupted Inez's memories. Glancing around, she said, "Now tell me: what's been happening?"

Listening to Inez describe her pains and watching her, Mrs. Snow said, "Let's get you in bed, where you'll be more comfortable." She helped Inez into her nightgown and smoothed the sheet for her. She said calmly, "The baby's early, although if it's determined to make an early entrance, we'll help it all we can. You're strong, and Dr. Simons has delivered hundreds of babies. He'll be here soon and help."

With that, she left the room to put the big copper tub filled with water on the cook stove and then added wood to the fire.

As the afternoon wore on, Mrs. Snow noticed the contractions were growing stronger and Inez's face and hair were becoming drenched with sweat. With each contraction coming only moments apart, Mrs. Snow knew it was nearing the time for the arrival of the baby. She took a sheet and tied it to the bedpost. The other end she handed to Inez. "Here, pull this when the pain comes, and it will help. The doctor should be along shortly."

Mrs. Snow glanced down as a big pool of water gushed out. The contractions were almost continuous now. With furrowed brow, she lit the lamps in the room. *Where is that doctor?* Mrs. Snow thought. *It seems he's had long enough to get here by now. I've been here well over three hours.*

Dr. Simons entered the room just as a little dark head appeared. Having washed his hands at the kitchen sink, he eased the tiny body from its safe place in her mother's womb. The baby was so tiny she was almost swallowed up by the doctor's large hands. She looked dark blue, there was no cry, and she wasn't breathing.

He spanked her, but she still wasn't breathing. Laying her down, he took a syringe from his bag and cleared her tiny throat. What took only moments to accomplish seemed like hours. Turning her upside down, he gave her another good spank. Moments seemed suspended in air, and then the baby gave a feeble little cry.

After he breathed a sigh of relief, the doctor did the preliminaries and handed the baby over to Mrs. Snow to be cleaned up and rubbed with oil. "That certainly didn't take you very long, Inez," he commented. "It must be because the baby is so small; she weighs in at just under two pounds."

"Oh thank God. I have my little girl. She's tiny, but she looks like she's determined." Inez smiled contentedly as she dropped off to sleep.

Dr. Simons entered the kitchen where Israel was pacing. "Well, you have a baby girl!" As Israel started to grin, the doctor went on, "I'm not sure she'll make it, though. She weighed in at just one pound, eleven ounces."

Israel felt his heart stop. He didn't know how Inez would be able to stand it if something happened to her little girl. "How can a baby that small make it?"

"She's alive now. That, in itself, is a miracle, but in the next few hours we will know if she will survive."

"We both were counting on this baby so much. Is Inez all right?" Israel asked the doctor with trepidation, afraid for any more bad news.

"She's doing fine, but very tired just now. I didn't tell her of the baby's danger. She's been through enough and I thought it best to wait awhile, 'til she's stronger. She's as weak as a kitten just now. Perhaps you can tell her when she wakes." The doctor then slipped out to return to Middleville to catch a few hours of sleep before his busy schedule began the next day.

Mrs. Snow brought the baby into the kitchen and put her in a laundry basket beside the wood stove. Israel slept in the kitchen rocker; Inez, in the four poster bed his father made them as a wedding present, just three short years earlier.

Throughout the night Mrs. Snow warmed flannel baby blankets on the stove and wrapped the tiny little girl snuggly in them, keeping her vigil, praying, changing the blankets for warm ones as each one cooled, rubbing life into the baby each time she changed her. All night she kept it up, never tiring, with a peaceful angelic look on her face.

As the first light of dawn appeared it seemed to the woman that the baby was growing pinker, and she slept more peacefully than before. "Dear God, I do believe she's responding. Thank You for this kind mercy." Mrs. Snow whispered with wonder and awe in her voice.

A few hours later Mrs. Snow brought the baby to Inez. The sun was just peeking over the hill. Inez's little bundle looked much better. Mrs. Snow had Inez squeeze some milk from her breast into a cup and then gave her an eyedropper to feed the little one with.

"Of all the years I've helped bring babies into the world, I've never seen such a small one survive. She's an amazing baby." Mrs. Snow said.

Israel cracked the door and peered in. Eyes still heavy from sleep, he walked over and knelt down by the bed, relief flooding his face at the sight of his much healthier daughter. "Is she all right?"

"She'll make it. She's tough little thing," responded Mrs. Snow with pride. Israel stared at the small bundle. "Would you like to hold her?" Inez asked, holding the baby up for him. He took her, and in amazement said, "Why, her head is so small I believe it would fit in a tea cup!"

Dr. Simon drove up the drive and hitched his horse to the hitching post. The rain had ended during the night; it was a beautiful morning. Israel was up the hill plowing the field for the planting of corn. The doctor hoped that was a good sign as he entered the back door and scraped his shoes on the boot brush. Mrs. Snow was in the kitchen making the baby dresses smaller. "Good morning, Dr. Simon. I thought I would stay around until Genie Hill gets here. Her brother Lonzo is bringing her today. She'll stay until Inez is on her feet."

"Is the baby still alive then?"

"She's alive and seems to be doing just fine."

"I can't believe it. Last night I didn't think she could possibly make it, she was so small," Dr. Simon said in amazement.

Inez beamed as the doctor entered the room. "We named her Clara Helen she has such bright eyes we thought she needed a sparkling name. Clara Helen Haff, born June the 3rd, 1905," she said proudly.

"Well look at you two," he said. Taking the baby, he put her on the foot of the bed to examine her. "I do believe she'll make it. I wouldn't have given two cents for her life last night." He watched as Inez changed from glowing to a worried expression.

"We'll just have to watch her closely, you understand? Make sure she stays warm and nurses well. She won't take much at one time so you will need to feed her more often. We'll just take it one day at a time. Send Israel for me at the slightest provocation. I'll check in tomorrow to see how she's doing. I know she'll get plenty of love and I've seen that pull a baby through when nothing else would."

Taking her precious bundle from him, Inez carefully held Clara to her breast. "And don't forget prayer, Doctor. God honors our requests." Tears of thanksgiving fell as she silently thanked the Lord for her miracle.

That afternoon Israel came down from the field, entered the house, and greeted Lonz and Genie, Inez's step brother and sister, who were in the kitchen drinking the iced tea Mrs. Snow had made for them to cool off after a long ride. "Well, I see you decided to come in and tend to your family," Aunt Genie snipped.

"Now leave him alone," Uncle Lonz implored. "He's trying to manage his family and the farm too!"

Aunt Genie, who was Inez' stepsister and almost twenty years older, had never been married and was "down on men," although no one really knew why. She earned a living working for people who could afford a housekeeper and spent her off time traveling from relative to relative "visiting" and, as Israel said, by making a penny stretch as far as a dollar managed to do quite well.

Uncle Lonz and Israel sat on the front porch rocking and having an amiable conversation. The world seemed at peace. Inez and Clara were both doing well. Everything looked bright and beautiful after the rain. "Say Israel," Lonz said, "you'll be needing to build a barn come fall by the look of that one." The present barn stood on the hillside looking run-down and dilapidated and much too small for Israel's purposes.

"Yes I will need it. Come fall I'll have no place big enough to store the crops and house the animals."

"I think there are enough men around to help you. It shouldn't take over a couple of days."

"Sounds like a good plan to me. Maybe attach a shed for Inez' chickens. She sure knows how to get maximum production out of them. She's using her egg money for material for clothes next winter."

"She's something, alright."

"She's also thinking of purchasing a flock of geese. She's full of plans. Between the two of us we hope to have a fully operational farm in five years. I pray things work that way."

As the sun sank behind the hill and the moon emerged in the sky, the two men sat rocking contentedly, each in their own thoughts.

Chapter 2

AS THE DAYS PASSED Inez' garden grew. Her prize dahlias stood proudly at the edge of her garden and were doing amazingly well. Announcing August, the dahlias, now in bloom, were the size of dinner plates and a blaze of color. The season found them a little short of rain so Inez faithfully carried water up the hill from the creek to water her garden. There was no way for Israel to water his crops and he was worried. The corn should have been knee high by the fourth of July, as the old saying goes, and it was far from it. They were depending on these crops to get the animals through the winter.

Inez finished hoeing the row of vegetables and paused a minute to watch Clara in her pram on the edge of the garden, staring at the trees visible to the right of the farm. She wondered what Clara could be thinking --- was she thinking about the time when she would be old enough to climb them? What does a two month old baby think of? She was such a good baby and she looked like a China doll. Her complexion was like peaches and cream and her hazel eyes snapped with interest at everything she looked at. Clara certainly had filled out nicely. She still was a little thing though, and still wearing the clothes Mrs. Snow had so graciously made smaller for her, although they would soon need to be replaced.

Thinking of that, Inez smiled at the pride Mrs. Snow had in Clara. Why, one would think it was all Mrs. Snow's doing, this little person of Clara, but she was the best- hearted woman Inez knew and she credited her with saving her baby's life. She looked up the hill to the Snow farm and was thankful they were neighbors.

As the summer passed, the crops were a little sparse. The property was sloped on the side of the hill and there were plateaus, but they drained too fast. Israel faithfully tilled the soil, worried, and prayed.

Inez would be able to can quite a bit of her garden produce. Throughout the rest of the summer she carried water from the creek, watered her garden and managed to save it. She worried about Israel, though. This was the first summer he was able to plant more of his acreage. In the past summers his time was spent clearing land. The farm had been sadly neglected before they purchased it.

Clara seemed to thrive with the fresh air and sunshine. Her little limbs were filling out nicely and her rosy cheeks glowed and bright eyes shone. Inez spent every possible moment outside with her and she accompanied her parents on their evening walks most of the time.

Aunt Genie was still with them and heartily disapproved of so much fresh air for Clara. She was sure the baby would catch pneumonia or worse and that it would be the death of her.

The morning that the Haff's relatives and neighbors were coming to build the new barn was finally upon them. The lumber had been delivered from town and was piled out by where the barn was to be.

Cyrus and Altie, Israel's brother and his wife had already arrived with their three girls, all the way from Grand Rapids. They were followed soon by Uncle Lonz and his wife Iva with their boys Lloyd, William, and Raymond and daughter Alice.

Iva and Alice entered the big kitchen laden with pies and casseroles for the noon meal. Alice unloaded and headed for Clara in the wicker buggy in the corner.

"Oh she's just the sweetest baby I've ever seen," Alice exclaimed, picking Clara up.

Clara giggled and rewarded her with a big smile. At fourteen years old, every baby was sweet to Alice, but she was right about Clara; she was mighty sweet.

Cyrus and Altie's girls, Fay, Fern and Evelyn, turned to look on with envy, wishing they had thought first of picking up the baby.

Grandma Martha sat in the corner presiding over the women. No longer able to do the physical work, she sat with knitting needles in hand working up the cutest little yellow bunting for Clara which would come in handy in the fall.

Clara was the first baby to come along in a while in this family, and therefore many wonderful gifts lay unopened in the corner. Opening gifts would have to come later. Now the tables were being filled up fast with tantalizing food.

Grandma Sarah, Israel's mother, not to be outdone, was working up a baby quilt which was something of a prize. "Clara will be the best dressed baby in all of Parmalee," Inez declared. Inez's niece Ellen, who she called sister as she was like a sister, looked on with pride in her new niece. Ellen's heart was filled with gladness for Inez and her budding family.

Israel came into the kitchen for more coffee from the big enamel pot. "Oh my, the smells in this kitchen are almost too much! I'll tell the men what we have to look forward to. That will keep us working hard." The kitchen was nearly busting at the seams with all the activity. Aunt Altie and Aunt Iva were chatting, busily cutting up chickens to be fried. The smell of tantalizing roast filled the room. Fay and Fern were busy making noodles. Biscuits and corn bread would be made at the last minute. Tables were being set up outside with various tablecloths for food.

Israel made his exit and returned to the barn site to help with the framing. With the help of family and neighbors the barn was already well in progress. Israel felt blessed indeed to have such great support.

The smell of the freshly cut wood along with the smell of ripening hay in the mid-morning sun gave him a strong sense of peace. He felt very fortunate to have such loyal friends and family. The young men were working hard to outdo one another. The floors and framing would be completed by noon, and the afternoon would be spent on the siding and roofing. As the men nailed the last trestle into place Inez came up the hill and rang the dinner bell. They all headed for the outdoor pump to wash. There was a great deal of good-natured splashing and jostling around. They had grown hot and the cool water felt good.

After the noon meal was finished, the women sat outside with needlework and visited while the men finished the barn. Ellen sat next to Inez holding Clara. As Inez glanced at Ellen she noticed her complexion was rosy with the sunshine and her eyes fairly glowing. "You look the picture of a rose bud," Inez remarked. "What's new in your life little sister?"

Ellen blushed and smiled, "Well," she lowered her voice and said, "John Shaw ask me to marry him."

"You still have a year to go before you finish school, Ellen."

"Well, we would like a year or so to plan and make arrangements. There's so much to be done."

"I think it is wonderful! I've seen him at church and he seems like a good person to me, and very attractive, too. Doesn't his father have the big corner farm, the one with the big red brick house?"

"Yes, that's theirs. He has a nice family, too--three brothers and two sisters. Two siblings are married and the other three are still home. I love him, Inez, and I know he's right for me."

Israel came walking down the hill. "Inez, got any more iced tea for some very thirsty men?"

"Oh mercy, time has gotten away from me! I'll bring some up right away."

As Inez and Ellen trudged up the hill with large pitchers full of iced tea, the men stopped to take a break and refresh themselves. The barn was nearing completion and the women were free with their praise.

It was a grand specimen of workmanship. After the men packed up all their tools and the women their dishes, Inez and Israel stood in their driveway saying good-bye to all their relatives, friends, and neighbors.

Holding Clara and surveying the farm, both of them feeling very happy and content. Israel said, "Well, I need to do the evening chores."

"I'll fix supper while you do that. Clara is so tired after a day of being passed around. It won't take her long to fall asleep." Israel head for the barn and Inez took Clara into the house.

Fall was upon them, the crops were in and, although sparse, would last the winter hopefully. Nights were cooler and days were shorter and leaves were turning shades of gold. Inez loved the smells of fall. Aunt Genie had returned home. Their family walks were pleasing and they enjoyed gathering the nuts they found along the way. Clara shared the walks, she took everything in along the way. Inez had made a back- pack for carrying Clara. They gathered wild berries for decoration for the holidays and made plans for those days ahead. Money was scarce, but love abounded, and they felt wealthy with all they had and especially the love they shared.

Chapter 3

THE WINTER PASSED WITHOUT much excitement. At Christmas, they all went to Grand Rapids to visit relatives there. They settled in for winter days and long winter nights with darkness coming so soon. Clara seemed to catch one cold after another. Mrs. Snow stopped by when she could get through the snow.

One morning in February Inez awoke with a start to Clara coughing. Crossing the cold wooden floor in her bare feet, she felt her baby's forehead. Clara was very warm to the touch. Clara had had several sore throats and respiratory infections since Christmas. Pouring water from the pitcher into the bowl on the commode, Inez bathed and quickly dressed, then combed her long, auburn hair into a bun on the nape of her neck.

Wrapping Clara warmly in blankets, Inez carried the baby down to the kitchen, laying her into the baby basket by the cook stove in the kitchen. She stirred the embers and put in wood to warm the kitchen and fix breakfast. Then she picked Clara up to feed her in the big rocker. Clara would only try to nurse a moment and then give up, fussing all the while. Inez closed her eyes and prayed silently, *Dear Lord you've been so good to us. Everything we've asked for Clara you've done. Once more I'm coming to you asking for you to watch over her. Help us to make good decisions on what we should do now. If we need Dr. Simons, please help us to find him easily and then help him to be wise in his care of her.*

Israel came into the kitchen from chores as Inez finished preparing the meal. "I believe we're in for a big snow storm," he commented as he sat down to breakfast. He gave thanks for the meal and Inez told him the concern she felt for the baby.

"The snow is already piling up," he said. "Do you think maybe we should send for Dr Simons now, before we have trouble getting him here? Mr. Snow is going to town this morning to fill a prescription for Mrs. Snow. If I get over to his place right away I can catch him before he leaves and have him ask the doctor to come out here."

"Yes, it might be a good idea, before the snow piles up so high that he can't get through from town. Hopefully the doctor is still in town. I know there are a couple of babies due now."

The kitchen was warm from the cook stove fueled from breakfast. Taking advantage of the warmth, Inez bathed Clara in cool water to bring down the fever.

Israel sat at the window and watched the snow pile up as he looked for the doctor, his painting untouched. Dressing Clara warmly, Inez sat in the rocker with Clara and tried to nurse her again. She wasn't really interested in eating, but Inez was able to get a little bit down her throat. The waiting seemed endless. The clock on the mantle ticked slowly, and time dragged by.

"Even if I tried to find the doctor it would be nearly impossible. No telling where he is," Israel said.

"Yes and we surely can't take Clara out in this. I guess we'll just have to do the hard thing and wait." Finally, Clara slept fitfully in Inez's arms. She put the baby into the basket, put her apron on, and said, "I guess I'll do some baking. That way I'll keep the kitchen nice and warm for Clara-- anything to make the waiting easier."

Finally, Israel saw Dr. Simons making his way up the driveway. Tying his horse to the hitching post, the good doctor waded his way through the snow, which had piled up considerably by then.

Israel made for the back door and opened it as the doctor came up to it. "Thank God you made it, Doctor!"

Entering the kitchen, the Dr. Simons asked Inez for Clara's symptoms. Opening his bag and taking out a thermometer, Dr. Simmons had Inez take off Clara's diaper and turn her on her stomach. Taking the instrument from her bottom and reading he commented, "We have a sick little girl on our hands. All indications that I can see show that there is an inflammation of the mastoid which is giving us the trouble. See how swollen it is here behind her ear?" As he touched the baby behind her ear she cried out in pain. "It's also very sore to the touch. I believe that's our problem."

"What does that mean? What can we do for her, Doctor?" Israel sighed.

"What I recommend is surgery. She is still so small for that, but these infections don't seem to be going away and each one will wear her down a little more," he said as he glanced at the worried parents. "I fear for her life if we don't do something soon. I would want to take her to Caledonia to the hospital there for the operation. I would like to be there to have use of all the equipment. She'll have the best of care at the hospital."

Inez and Israel nursed and fussed over Clara until the latest crisis with her illness was over. Once Clara was well enough, arrangements were made to take her to the hospital as soon as the current infection cleared up.

The following week Inez bundled Clara up in warm blankets, and Israel brought the buggy around to the back door. They drove the long miles in silence, but with much prayer.

At the hospital, after a night of observation and rest, the nurses prepared Clara to be taken into surgery. The parents watched, feeling helpless, as the attendants took baby Clara down the corridor. "She looks so small and defenseless," Israel commented. At eight month old Clara was still small for her age and so little to be taken all alone on the large sterile-looking gurney. She looked at her parents as if to say, "What are you doing to me?"

Meeting them in the hall to surgery Dr. Simon explained, "I will be performing a mastoidectomy by making an incision behind her right ear to remove infected cells. Ether will be carefully administered by a nurse and when Clara wakes up she will be watched closely for a few days to be sure no infection develops and, of course, we'll watch her progress."

"Will she be okay, Doctor?" Inez asked, knowing he didn't know the answer.

"Just pray, Inez," he said.

And so it was that Inez and Israel sat quietly in the waiting room feeling helpless. They held hands and prayed, putting Clara in God's hands, and gathered strength for the outcome. The waiting seemed endless. It was difficult to imagine their small girl undergoing such surgery, but they felt that God didn't bring them this far just to let them down.

"We've come so far with Clara, through so much, I just can't stand the thought of losing her now," Israel said.

"I'm glad we've had her this long, whatever happens," Inez said bravely.

"Yes, that's true."

A kind Red Cross worker came into the room and offered them coffee.

Inez asked if the surgery would be over soon. "You need to settle back and relax as best you can. It will be awhile before it's over," the Red Cross said. After that they did relax more and read from the worn Bible Israel had with him. The Psalms seemed to come to life for them in view of what they were facing. The promises made to David so many ages ago seemed to be written for them just now. They prayed together and committed Clara's life to God. At first it had been hard for them to fully give their treasured baby's life to Him, but they came to realize hands more capable then theirs were needed, and God's trusted hands were the only place they would find complete peace in any circumstance.

It was a haggard-looking Doctor who came out of surgery several hours later. He plopped himself into a chair opposite the parents and announced that it had been a successful operation and Clara would be sleeping for some time yet. "Mind you, we're not out of the woods yet. Her developments in the next few hours should tell us more, but, she is alive and seems to be doing alright," he said cautiously.

They were taken to the window of the recovery room where they watched Clara take shallow breaths, thankful to see her alive. They prayed a prayer of gratitude and Inez said "anything God does is well done."

Later that day Israel left to return home and care for the stock. It was very lonely, leaving his family at the hospital and coming home to an empty house.

Inez stayed with Clara and watched her all through the night. Soon after the sun peeked over the horizon Clara aroused herself. She looked so small and fragile. The nurses and Inez took such good care of her that she gained strength all the time and in a few days was able to go home.

The following week Israel drove in horse and buggy to Caledonia to pick up his girls. Clara was much more herself again, and sat on Inez lap bundled in heavy blankets enjoying every mile. It was a beautiful, unseasonably warm afternoon. The sun was shining and the snow-covered branches glistened. Clara giggled as she watched two squirrels chasing each other up a tree. Coming up on the farm Inez had a deep sense of promised peace; her baby was going to be alright. The doctor had cautioned her to watch Clara carefully. "I'll be out to see her daily for a few days," he said.

One evening, a few weeks later, Inez decided to have a quilting bee to make Ellen a wedding quilt. "We haven't gotten together, and it's been such a long winter. I think when there's a break in the weather I'll send word around and invite everyone," she told Israel.

It was the end of March before the quilting bee could take place, but they were all there—Inez's friends and neighbors all wishing Ellen well. The snow was melting and pussy willows were showing their fuzzy heads. The farm women seemed to gain strength from the smell and sight of spring in the air. They all had plans of how they would make their gardens the talk of the countryside. The women chatted and worked together to create a beautiful quilt for the coming wedding.

Chapter 4

INEZ AND CLARA—NOW TWO years old—walked up the hill behind
the Haff farm. Clara was still small for her age but she was bright
and full of questions, particularly about nature. She loved the
farm animals and observed them all. She would walk up to the birds
and reach out her hand to them, only to have them fly away. Looks
disappointment and bewilderment crossed her face; all she wanted to do
was be friendly and pet them, but they didn't seem to understand. The
barn cat, and especially the kittens and baby animals, were delightful
with her, and she couldn't comprehend the difference between them
and the wild animals. She could name all the animals and make their
sounds. She liked to "talk" to them in their language. She loved to roll
with the collie. Today, she was looking forward to seeing her daddy.

Inez had a pitcher of lemonade for Israel, who had been cultivating
corn all morning. It was springtime again, and they were expecting their
second child soon. The sky was a heavenly blue, the birds were singing,
and the earth had a clean fresh smell. Life was good.

Israel saw them coming and stopped at the end of the row. "What
are you up to, Katura?" For some reason this pet name he had for
Clara caught on, and he often used it. Clara, with her round little legs
and shiny, honey colored hair toddled over to her Daddy to give him a
present. Daddy smiled down at Clara as she smiled up at him with her
glistening hazel eyes. With delight she handed him her present, then
looked at it with regret. "This is wonderful, Clara-- thank you--but
will you take care of it for daddy for now?" With a smile, she eagerly
accepted the worm back.

Israel took a long cool drink of lemonade and, as he leaned on the cultivator to rest a moment, he asked Inez, "Did I see the mailman leave a letter?"

"Yes, we just got a letter from Aunt Genie, and she plans to be here next Tuesday, if the weather holds out, and will help as long as we need her."

"Wonderful! That really puts my mind at ease. How are you feeling now, Inez? You look a little tired." She would be delivering soon. The garden was in, and things were starting to peek through the ground already. The house was scrubbed from top to bottom with curtains clean and crisp. The pantry was stocked, the canning shelves still held ample supply. She was ready for the baby's arrival.

"I'm a little tired Israel, but things are pretty much in order, so I should be able to take it a little easy from now on. There was so much to do for Ellen's wedding but now that she is happily married, we should be able to settle into a routine. How is the corn crop looking?" she asked, changing the subject.

"Well it seems to be missing something. It's just not where I think it should be. I'm not sure what, though. Maybe I'll talk to Lonz when he's here with Aunt Genie."

That June Inez presented them with their long-awaited son, Francis, and then the following year Walter, and then two years later, Forest.

Israel was, for the most part, a happy man. Clara was the apple of his eye, always bright and sparkling. His three sons would grow up to be partners in his farming business, and he had the love and support of his wife. Something still nagged him about the farm, though, he just couldn't seem to get really good production out of the land.

People advised different methods of boosting the nutrients of the soil, but nothing really seemed to help all that much. Inez was busy and happy with her young family, though she did worry about her husband. Anything that affected Israel also affected her.

Clara was always busy and Francis and Walter were right behind her. Baby Forest was really the serious one in the family. Fat and dimpled, his eyes followed his siblings always with an inquisitive look on his face. He seemed to be saying, "What are you three up to now?"

Aunt Genie was a frequent visitor and pretended outrage at all the goings on of the children. Deep down, she loved them and enjoyed their zest for life.

The family had just settled down for the night with a good breeze that would bring rain with it to lull them to sleep. Israel woke about three o'clock to strong bolts of lightning and thunder. As he lay there, the storm seemed to be getting closer. He rose from the bed and went to the window just in time to see a large bolt of lightning hit the barn. The timber in the barn ignited. Israel ran for the door, his pants in hand. Inez followed right behind him. "Inez, stay here with the children and Aunt Genie," he told her. They both noticed windows in the Snow's house light up at the same time. "He'll alert the other neighbors," Israel said.

He grabbed buckets from the back shed on his way out the door and headed for the creek to fill them. Before long, enough men for a fire brigade arrived. They passed water from the creek to douse the barn.

Israel ran to get the stock from within. A few men followed and worked with him to get the animals out safely. The horses, fearing the flames, stubbornly dug their heels into the floor. It took several strong men to get them out. After the horses were out, the men carried newborn pigs out of the barn, and the sow trotted after her litter. Working diligently, they finally cleared the barn of all the livestock. The flames had gone from the roof down to the main floor. Fearing that the barn would collapse on them, the men stood back and watched the fire destroy the timber of the barn built just six years ago. Before morning, the barn was leveled.

The sun came out brilliantly the next morning, and all nature had a peaceful aura about it, belying the destruction of the previous night. This was indeed a discouraging day in the life of the Haff's.

All the friends and neighbors were gone, and Israel and Inez stood with Clara at the foot of the hill where the barn once stood. The barn was their one real accomplishment, besides their family, of which they were proud.

Clara, hearing a sound, looked under a little pile of building material, and there was mother cat cleaning a new batch of kittens delivered during the night. "Oh Mommy, look! Here are my kittens! That fire didn't get them," she cried as she stooped over to see them. Israel and Inez smiled to each other at the small miracle. "I guess life goes on" Inez remarked.

"Thank God the crops are still in the fields," Israel said.

"Thank God you were able to get the animals out safely," Inez said.

"They'll be able to stay out to pasture for a while if the weather holds. I'll just round up the cows at milking time."

That day the family took stock of where they were and what the next step would be. They encouraged each other and were thankful it was the barn and not the house and that the family was safe and no one had been hurt. "I guess we have many things to be thankful for after all," Israel remarked.

After a restless night and breakfast to give him courage, Israel left the house to see what, if anything, could be saved. Halfway up the hill he heard horse's hooves. He turned and saw riders coming from every direction. The first one to reach him was his new brother-in-law, John Shaw. "We're here to clear up this mess and build a new barn, brother." Other men came up then and seemed determined to get to work. Israel's eyes were moist with gratitude. One week later a new barn had been erected.

A few days later, Clara had been sent out to play and watch Walter, who wouldn't have let Clara out of his sight anyway. The new litter of kittens were a few weeks old now and at a most playful stage. Clara was enjoying them and laughing at their antics when she realized her brother was missing. She looked and looked and couldn't find him, so she got up her courage and ran in to tell Mama. Inez came flying out of the kitchen to join the search. She looked in and around the barn and didn't see him anywhere, then ran down to the dreaded creek and peered into the water. Not finding him there, she breathed a sigh of relief, walking up and down the length of the property after searching the creek. There was no sign of him anywhere. She happened to look back in the barn, and there was two-year-old Walter on the top floor of the barn, looking down and grinning proudly at Inez. "Stay where you are Walter and don't move! I'll be right there to get you." Up to the loft she climbed and walked quietly over to grab him.

"I pay hide and see," he wailed.

Inez took him into the house, spanked him, and gave him a hug and a fresh-baked cookie. "Walter, never climb on the barn ladder again and stay with Clara while you're outdoors playing. You might get hurt, and Mommy would be very sad. Do you understand?" He nodded that he understood and tearfully took a bite of cookie.

That night, as Inez prepared for bed, she recounted the story to Israel.

"I guess we can count our blessings all around, can't we?" He said.

"Yes, the Lord certainly does look out for us. We must remember to thank Him tonight!"

Chapter 5

I N THE FALL ISRAEL went to an auction of farm animals to purchase a hog to breed with his sows in the spring. As he sat there a very good specimen was brought to the platform. The bidding was just getting started when he made a bid. "I wouldn't do that if I were you," remarked his brother-in-law. "That animal belongs to old Jim Blake up the hill from me, and I know for a fact that he is mean. He charged after the neighbors' boy when he tried to cut through his field--nearly caught him too!"

"Well, maybe I can get the hog for a good price. I'll breed it next spring and then butcher it," Israel replied, thinking of their diminishing resources. "It looks like a fine bull to me, one I can afford. I'll just make sure I secure him well."

The group of men remained quiet as the auctioneer encouraged them to bid. Israel commented sheepishly, "Well I still think it's a good buy. I'll just build a strong fence to keep him in. He won't be able to bust out of it."

So the hog was brought home and securely fenced up. "Clara, don't go near that pen," he warned, "and keep the boys away from it, too."

That Thanksgiving it was their turn to have dinner at the Haff home. Mid-morning, people started arriving. Ellen and John arrived first. "Clara, look at you! You look so pretty in that dress Mommy made you." Turning to Inez, she said, "Inez, red does seem to be her color." She knelt to give Clara a big hug.

"Aunt Ellen, we got a new pig, but he's mean and we can't play with him," Clara announced importantly.

"Well, be sure to stay away from him then," Ellen warned. "I wouldn't want to see any of my favorite nephews or my niece hurt."

"Francis, you're getting so big I hardly recognize you!" she commented as she hugged him. "Oh, and look at Walter," she said as he came running to her for a hug. Then, picking up the baby, she nestled him into her neck. "Forest, you are the sweetest baby I know." She gave him a kiss on the cheek and lifted him in the air. "Speaking of babies, Inez," Ellen said, "guess who will be joining our household next spring!"

"No--don't tell me! I think he'll have a cousin about the same age to play with!" Inez replied. The two 'sisters' hugged each other with joy.

In the living room John was busy looking at Israel's artwork. "You really should sell some of this. It's very good, Israel!"

"No, I really wouldn't feel right parting with them. They're so much a part of us. Besides, if I had gone to art school it would be worth money, but as it is, they are not worth much of anything to anyone else but us."

"Well I don't agree. I think they're very good." By then more of the family had arrived and the subject was changed.

Chloe, Israel's sister, was visiting from up north, and his sister Aunt Rilla and Uncle Ernest were in from Charlotte.

Big tables were set up from the kitchen through into the living room. Inez had dressed two of her biggest turkeys. Besides potatoes and gravy, there were assorted vegetables, salads, rolls and pies. Aunt Rilla made her special cranberry relish and Chloe brought along her wonderful gelatin salad with fruit and whipped cream. She even brought a special little bowl for Francis because he didn't like fruit in his. Dinner was wonderful; such a feeling kinship and belonging existed among the family.

Later the women were in the kitchen clearing and washing dishes and talking about the produce they had accumulated for the winter in fruit cellars. The men were comparing crops they had stored in the barns. The boys were taking afternoon naps, and Clara was out playing with the collie, Taffy. She ran after him, chasing him around the barn, and then it was his turn to chase.

On and on they ran until Clara paused to look at the new hog they had been warned to stay away from. As she stood looking at him he looked back and gave a little snort. *He looks like he's lonely,* she thought. *All the other animals like me. I think he does, too. He almost looks like he's smiling at me.* The hog snorted again and went to the other side of the pen. Clara called him over to her, and he came partway and just stood there looking at her. She crawled under the fence and walked about halfway to where he was standing. He kicked up his heels and ran toward her.

Clara ran as fast as her short legs could carry her, but all the while the animal was closing in on her. Three feet from the fence he butted her with all his force. She fell as she reached the fence and her head crashed against it. Satisfied, the pig walked away.

Clara opened her eyes to see Mama and Daddy hugging each other and crying. All the relatives crowded around the bed sobbing. "Look she's alive!" Uncle Ernest cried.

Then the sobs really broke out. As Doctor Simons arrived and examined her, he said that she received a mild concussion from the hard fall against the fence. "She's a very lucky little girl."

That afternoon they sat down for dessert, all very relieved that Clara would be okay.

Israel looked at Inez and said, "I think we should give thanks for another blessing today, along with our food. Our heavenly Father is truly watching over us."

As Christmas neared, the house became alive with excitement. The smells of the holiday were permeating everything. The children were so full of energy it was hard to keep them still. Clara and the boys were bundled up and they trudged out behind Daddy to the sleigh waiting for them at the back door. Daddy grabbed toddler Forest as he fell toward a snow bank and swung him up to the seat beside Israel. Clara, Francis and Walter were put in the back seat and tucked in with furry blankets. They were on their way to find a Christmas tree.

About a mile down the road they came to some sparse woods. Israel had spotted an excellent tree two years before and watched it grow to just the right size, but pretended to look for the perfect tree with the children.

They all climbed out of the sleigh and went scurrying toward the woods. As he headed the children toward the tree so as to accidentally find it, Clara saw the saddest looking tree yet! "Oh look, I think that one wants to come home with us," she cried.

Francis looked at it with suspicion. "We couldn't string very much popcorn on those branches. There aren't enough of them," he said.

"But it looks so lonely out here all alone," Clara said. "Daddy can't we take this one, please?"

"Why don't we leave it for a year or two until it grows up and fills out some,' Israel suggested. Hesitating, Clara agreed to wait one more year. Then they came upon the tree Israel had secretly selected. Israel hesitated, hoping someone would spot it, but there was only silence. "Well, what about this one? It seems about the right size for our parlor. You know Mama warned us about getting one too large," he encouraged.

The children all agreed finally that it was the right size and would hold plenty of decorations. So it was cut down and loaded on the back of the sleigh.

As they returned home, Mama was waiting at the back door to take their wet garb to dry by the kitchen stove.

Israel set the tree up while Inez finished beef stew in the kitchen. Steaming apple pie sat on the sideboard cooling.

After supper, the tree was decorated as they sang Christmas carols. Cranberries and popcorn garlands were strung and candles were carefully placed. An angel that had been made by Grandma Sarah adorned the treetop. Walter was lifted up to place it on the top, and then the children were carried off to bed.

Inez and Israel sat and reminisced about their day. While he was out with the children finding the perfect tree, she had been busy wrapping the packages they had so lovingly made for their family. Life was so good; God was surely with them.

Chapter 6

"Clara, when you use your pencil, put it in your other hand, like this. You should write with your right hand," her teacher instructed. Clara really got along well with her teacher, Mrs. Burgess. She didn't know why she was having trouble with this. She usually was able to do everything well and please Mrs. Burgess.

Clara put the pencil in her right hand and tried to make the different shapes in her penmanship book. *I wonder why this feels so funny. I just can't do it good with this hand. I don't know why,* she thought.

"You just keep trying Clara. You'll get it!" Mrs. Burgess firmly believed if Clara practiced she could write as well with her right hand as with her left.

Finally the school bell rang, and Clara could leave the writing behind for now. Out into the sunshine she went, glad for her freedom. Doris Snow, her nearest neighbor, always walked home with her. She was especially pleased with the company this afternoon so she wouldn't have to think of her writing. The sun was shining after all the rain they had yesterday. The air was crisp and clean and the bark on the trees was dark and fresh with the leaves of the trees baring yellow, red, burnt orange, dark red, green, and every other shade of fall. Clara kicked the leaves as she walked along. She so loved the sound of them. The smell of fall was so pleasing to her, like sweet, nutty, fragrant perfume.

Doris was two years older than Clara and seemed to know everything. "Your Mama's going to have another baby," she announced importantly.

"She isn't. She would have told me if she was going to have a baby before she told anyone else."

"But she is. I heard her talking about it to my mother when she was at my house Saturday. Don't you see how big her stomach is?"

By that time they were at the drive to the Haff farm and Doris had to leave. "I'll see you tomorrow," Clara called as she ran up the driveway to her house and burst through the back door. "Mama, are we really going to have a baby?" she cried breathlessly, setting her lunch pail on the table.

Inez stood at the ironing board and looked up, surprised. "Where did you get that idea?"

"Doris just said that we were."

"Sit down a minute Clara. I wanted to tell you myself and probably should have before, but yes, we are going to have a new baby. Now that you know we can make plans. You can help get everything ready. The baby will be here before we know it. So I'll need lots of help. Now run out in the back yard and get your brothers for milk and cookies. I hear Forest waking up from his nap. I'll go get him."

"Well, I sure wish we could have a baby girl this time," she said, running out the door.

Clara found her brothers playing down by the creek. They weren't allowed in it without an adult because the current was so swift, but they had poles with strings on them and were fishing.

"Hi Clara! We're trying to catch a fish but they won't bite our string. I can even see them down there!" Walter said.

"You need worms and a hook for that," Clara said importantly. "Mama said to come and have milk and cookies with us."

Clara was a big help for Mama getting ready for the baby. She helped Mama fold the baby diapers and clothes and put them in the drawers after cleaning and lining them and she did a fine job scrubbing the baby pram and basket.

Israel finished harvesting the crops, picking apples, and digging potatoes. He didn't feel too badly about his crops. He felt they would make it through the winter at least.

They had snow by the second week of November. Inez carefully groomed her geese for market. She was really feeling pretty well as fall progressed into winter. This was their fifth baby and most of the blankets, sweaters and bunting still looked good, so Inez only had to sew up new clothes to replace the worn ones.

As all the provisions were stored away for winter, the family had more time together. One evening they sat by the fire together. Mama had just put Forest to bed. "I think this is a good night for a taffy pull," she said. "It's Friday, so there's no school for you tomorrow."

When the taffy was made and was cool enough to handle, they all helped pull it. Walter got more on him than he pulled and some managed to find its way to his mouth. They laid the long strands on wax paper on the table, and Mama cut some for them to eat. She would cut the rest up later. Then they made popcorn.

"Tell us the story about Grandma and Grandpa Haff coming to Michigan. Tell us about the time Grandpa got sick and the wagon accident," the kids begged their father.

"Will there be time before they need to go to bed, Inez?"

"If you don't go into so many details," she agreed.

"Father and Mother lived in Indiana on a small farm," Israel said. "They could hardly make a go of it. The house was small after Uncle Albert and Aunt Ester came along and there wasn't much room to raise crops. Then Father heard about land in Michigan that was being sold at a good price, that there was rich farmland to be had, and that the country was beautiful. He also heard that the new denomination of the Free Methodist Church was being established in Michigan. A man named B.T. Roberts had broken with the Episcopal Methodist, or rather, been expelled for preaching holy living, and formed the new denomination. The Free Methodist denomination interested your grandfather; he liked what they stood for."

"Why aren't we Free Methodist?" Clara wanted to know.

"Well, there isn't a Free Methodist church around here, so we're the next best thing, the Missionary church. That's a good church, too."

"Well anyway, they sold their cabin to a Quaker family, and after the crops were in at the end of September, they took the beds and table and chairs apart and loaded them into a wagon along with grain and supplies enough to last the winter. Then they were on their way.

"As it turned out, it rained for days and everything was a soggy mess. Your grandfather got sick along the way, which delayed the trip, and then they had to leave some things when a wheel got stuck in the mud and was broken. This took some time to be repaired. By the time they reached Stoney Point, near Hastings, winter was coming on pretty well, so they built a sod hut and lived in it until the spring thaw."

"How could they live in a hut all winter?" Francis wanted to know.

"They were really pretty comfortable, actually. They used dried cow chips, which they brought along with them from Indiana, for fire to keep warm and for fuel to cook with, and the snow piled up outside for insulation, so they stayed nice and warm."

"After that, Father built the house I grew up in. As the children came along he added bedrooms.

"They had four more children in Michigan," said Clara importantly, "Aunt Mary and then Daddy and Chloe, Cyrus, and Sarah."

"My brother and sisters all got married and moved away and then Grandpa died and Grandma and I lived there all alone until I married your Mother," Israel finished.

"Tell us about our Uncle Benjamin Franklin," Clara said.

"Well", said Father, glancing at Mother for approval, "he was your Grandmother Sarah's great, great uncle's son. Her Father, George Franklin lived in Hamilton, Ohio. Benjamin Franklin was a very wise man. You'll be reading about him in your history books."

The fire was dying down now and the children were growing sleepy. "Well children, it's time for bed now. Francis can hardly keep his eyes open. It's been a good evening."

"Just one more story please," Clara begged.

"Some other time, let's get you tucked in bed and prayers said," Inez said firmly.

Clara lay in the dark thinking how sad it would be when her family all grew and moved away. She hoped that day would be a long time in coming. After a while she started thinking about the new baby instead and decided in the morning she would ask Mama if she could name her

Lois. She had just been reading about Lois in the Bible and thought it was such a special sounding name. She thought Lois must have been pretty wise to teach Timothy all about the Bible. With this pleasant thought, Clara fell fast asleep.

The September rains came, and the creek swelled. One day Uncle Lonz and Aunt Iva came to visit with their children Alice, Lloyd, William, and Raymond.

While the adults visited, the children were playing down by the creek. The water was rushing by going someplace in a hurry. Raymond saw a large trout swim by just a couple feet from him. He stepped on a rock to catch it with a net, and the moss, made slippery by the new level of water from the heavy rains, caught him in the swiftly moving current. The children saw him being carried up under the bridge.

Francis bounded up the hill to get help. Clara darted across the road to see if she could see him. She just caught a glimpse of him as he was being carried every which way by the current. Clara picked up a big stick and yelled, "See if you can reach this." No luck! He was gasping so hard that he missed it and was carried on down the stream.

On and on he went with Clara running after him on the shore, praying silently all the time. Once his shirt billowed with air and seemed to slow him a bit. He came just inches from shore and Clara caught just a bit of his shirt. She almost lost it, but managed to get a better grip and grab his arm. With supernatural strength, she dragged her cousin from the water up the incline to shore.

The men came running up. Father turned the boy over, and Raymond started coughing. Finally short, shallow breaths came more easily. Uncle Lonz picked up his son, and a wet, silent group walked into the house a few minutes later. Raymond was put by the cook stove to warm up. Uncle Lonz rubbed Raymond's blue skin, and Inez got some warm dry clothes for him to put on.

Two hours later Raymond sat by the warm hearth covered with blankets. "Clara," Uncle Lonz said, looking at her in amazement, "I saw you pull him out of the stream. How did you possibly manage that? He weighs so much more than you do, and he was wet and full of water, and lifeless too!"

"I don't know. I just felt so strong, like someone else was helping me," she said as though she was also puzzled. They all felt this tremendous sense of peace surrounding them. It was one of the visits none of family would ever forget!

Chapter 7

CLARA OPENED HER EYES and heard her mother's cries. At first she was afraid, but then she soon realized that she had heard those cries before, and then she knew her mama was about to have her new baby sister (at least she hoped it was a girl). She washed and quickly dressed and bound down the stairs to the warm kitchen with the good breakfast smells.

Aunt Genie had come to stay with them shortly after Christmas because Mama wasn't feeling as well during this pregnancy. Aunt Genie had a good heart, Clara remembered Mama saying, but sometimes she was cross and would scold Clara, but she would usually give her a cookie afterwards. Still, Aunt Genie wasn't mama; she just wasn't mama.

This morning Clara was happy and comforted to know that Aunt Genie was in the kitchen, in charge, in control.

"Clara, come and get your breakfast. It will soon be time for school and you still have chores to do," Aunt Genie said curtly.

"But I can't go to school today! Mama's having a baby!"

"Oh yes you can young lady. You'll be better off in school with something to do rather than staying here getting in the way." Clara had learned that once Aunt Genie made up her mind there was no changing it, so she quickly ate her breakfast and went to feed Mama's chickens.

It was a very long day in school to be sure, but it finally ended, and Clara ran the whole way home.

She ran into the kitchen and she just knew there was a new baby. "Can I go see her? Can I?" she begged Aunt Genie.

"No, the baby isn't doing well and she needs to sleep!" Aunt Genie said, as a look of horror came across Clara's face.

"Oh, let her see the baby," Israel said. "We don't know long she will have."

Clara thought she knew what that meant, but she wouldn't let herself think about it.

Turning to her, Daddy said, "Clara, the baby has had a rough time, so I want you just to look at her now. When she's feeling better you can hold her."

"Daddy, did we really have a baby girl?" Clara's face was shining with pleasure.

They did name her Lois—Lois Ruby. She had a dark little head and such an angelic look about her. She went to be with God and His angels only a few short months later.

While she was here Clara came to love her so very much! She watched her baby sister's every move, but Lois wasn't meant to stay long on earth. She kept getting thinner and more wan-looking all the time. She didn't have an appetite and wasn't interested in much. She did love to nestle up to her family as they held her. It was kind of like she knew she wouldn't be with them long.

One night she just slipped away in her sleep. Clara felt so lost after that; everything seemed meaningless and empty. Everywhere Clara went Lois wasn't there.

Clara didn't think she would ever stop hurting. Mama looked so sad and didn't laugh anymore. Baby Forest became even more somber. Daddy worked a lot harder, but still Clara felt their love--maybe a little more--because each member of the family was treasured even more. They realized just how fragile and precious life was.

Clara vowed that when she grew up and had babies she would name her first daughter Lois. She spun her imagination even farther and thought maybe this Lois would name her grandson Timothy and would teach him to love God like Lois did in the Bible. Clara's daughter's middle name could be Christine which was Inez's middle name and the feminine version of her Grandfather, Peter Christian's, middle name, the one who came from Denmark on a cattle ship and was so sick that he barely made it.

Spring melted into summer with all the crops growing and flowers blooming. Summer brought warmth, sun, and long hot lazy days by the swiftly-flowing creek. Berry picking in the woods in the reviving weather seemed to bring a quiet peace to Mama, and therefore the whole family seemed to grow more like themselves again. The berry picking and helping Mama with jam seemed to work together to give Clara a healing balm also.

Daddy drew a small picture of Lois for Clara, and she put it on her wall to remember her baby sister. Clara talked to Lois at night when she said her prayers and asked God to kiss her baby sister goodnight. *I think I will always think of Lois and wonder what she looks like. Even now I can imagine how much she's grown. Maybe her hair is blond like Uncle Otis' and she has blue eyes like his. Well someday in Heaven I'll see her, and then I'll know how she looks,* Clara thought.

That fall, Francis started school and made life in school more interesting for Clara. She felt Mama gave her charge of her younger brother; she was very protective of him and made sure he got to and from school okay.

Chapter 8

CLARA STUCK HER HEAD out from under the covers and looked out her window which was covered with little crystals of ice forming a variety of pictures and prisms. The sun was casting its brilliance on them, giving Clara a thrill. They looked like the stained glass windows at church.

Her mother opened the door and glanced at Clara as she lay there with golden strains of hair spread on the pillow, her hazel eyes sparkling at the sight as she lay studying the window. Smiling to herself, Inez said, "Clara get up and dress quickly. Daddy's getting the horse and buggy ready to take you to school. It's too cold outside for you to walk."

Clara bounded from bed and felt the shock of the cold plank floor. To be driven to school on the horse and buggy was rare indeed and was very exciting. Walter, who was now in school also, brought an apple out to give the horse. Like Clara, Walter was an animal lover and they responded well to him. The horse eagerly accepted the offering of the apple. The kids got in and were bundled in blankets. They sang sleighing songs all the way to school. Clara heard her Father say it was 22 degrees below zero that morning.

The potbelly stove in the school nearly glowed with the hot fire. Clara felt warm and cozy and especially enjoyed school that morning. It was nice to have her two brothers in school with her.

The teacher, Mrs. Burgess, lent her books regularly for Clara to take home and read to her brothers or just to herself. One night, she lay reading by lamplight when her Mama came to turn it out. "Clara it's time to go to sleep now."

"Please let me read just to the end of the chapter," she begged.

"You need to get to sleep now so you won't be too tired tomorrow." Mama knew Clara wouldn't be able to stop with just one chapter.

When Mama left, Clara was so anxious to see what happened next that she went into Mama and Daddy's room and got the flashlight to finish the chapter. She read to the end of the book and after that night she read many more books with her head covered and the flashlight lighting the pages for her.

One day before Christmas the children came home from school to find Mama crying and plucking geese out on the chopping block. She had a whole pile of them.

"What are you doing, Mama?" Francis asked. "Why are you plucking all those geese?"

Daddy walked up just then and answered for her. "It looks like the whole flock just keeled over and died. We don't know why."

It was a pretty sad household that night. They were trying to decide how to use all those geese. "I will can some of them and give the rest to neighbors. I was counting on selling them in the spring, though, to earn money for material for new curtains and such. It's been so long since I've replaced them. I don't dare wash them many more times," Mama fussed.

Israel felt so badly for Inez that he thought of selling some of his paintings to give her the money, but then discounted the idea, not really believing he could make any money on them. Inez said she would make new feather pillows for everyone for Christmas. That, at least, was something to look forward to.

The next morning, as they were eating breakfast, Israel happened to look out the kitchen window. He started laughing uproariously.

"What's so funny, Israel? I don't see anything to laugh at," Inez wondered despondently.

"You just have to see this for yourself" he laughed, as she stepped to the window. The children really couldn't understand it when Mama started laughing too. At that point they all ran to see. There on the clothesline were the naked geese for the whole world to see. It seems they had gotten into some sour mash and got stone drunk! The geese had a pretty cold winter but huddled together and survived.

That spring Mama had another surprise. This time she told Clara before anyone else, (except Daddy of course) that they were going to have another baby in the fall. Again they hoped and planned. A little girl would be nice.

Another summer passed with minimal crop yield. Israel thought they would just get by again this year. Three tan little children trudged off to school, unhappy to have the summer end but happy to see their friends and teacher again. Clara was looking forward to having new books to read.

In October a new baby joined the family. It was a girl! She looked like a little rosebud, so they called her Rosemond. She had a beautiful china complexion with pink cheeks, dark wavy hair, and snappy brown eyes. Clara simply adored her. She was a spunky little thing and liked to have her own way. The whole family coddled her and allowed it.

Aunt Rilla and Uncle Ernest from Charlotte came to visit at Christmas, and Aunt Rilla seemed especially taken with the baby. "If I had a daughter of my own I would like her to be just like Rosemond!" she was heard to comment one time. Everyone did seem to adore the new baby girl.

Chapter 9

THINGS WENT ON PRETTY much the same for a time. Israel worked the soil, only to be disappointed again come harvest time. He plowed, added nutrients, read the Farmer's Almanac, worried, and still the farm never became a big producer. The summer Clara was eleven years old an event took place which would change the family's lives forever.

Clara had an inner feeling that her Mama wasn't quite the same anymore. Clara couldn't put her finger on it but Mama just seemed to go through her days ungratified, as if the joy had gone out of her. Inez hugged and loved her children, but it was like the pleasure was gone from her.

Clara came home from school one day and went to look for Mama. She found her in her bedroom, kneeling on her bed, worn Bible in front of her on the bed. Mama was crying!

"I'll be alright, Clara dear. I just needed a good cry," Inez told her daughter.

Another time Clara found her mama in the barn, on her knees again praying and crying. Sometimes Clara would hear Mama up very late working. Mama always looked so sad and tired the next morning. One night Clara, feeling that maybe Mama was burdened with too much work, came downstairs to see if she could help Mama with some of the work.

"I'm pretty big now, you know. I am eleven years old. It's time I started helping more and making things a little easier for you."

"Clara, you go to bed, you need your sleep for school tomorrow,"

Mama said despondently. Discouraged, Clara went back upstairs, a big knot in the pit of her stomach. She couldn't have explained it even if she tried and fell asleep feeling very heavy-hearted.

One day Inez told the family another baby would be coming in the fall. There didn't seem to be any thrill in it for Mama like there was when the other babies were born.

Clara helped her get ready for the baby, cleaning furniture and clothes. On the surface everything went on as before.

Rosemond was now two years old and loved by all. Daddy seemed to take a special delight in her. She toddled around and was into everything. The children took a certain pleasure in entertaining her also. Clara liked dressing her up and treating her like a doll. Her little sister was a very beautiful girl and Clara loved her so.

The boys, six, eight, and nine years old, were old enough to be a big help to their Father on the farm. They hoed the corn, fed the animals, and cleaned the barn. They were also a big help to Mama. They worked the garden, churned the butter, and were available to help with general labor.

Walter took special delight in the farm and in seeing things grow. He liked picking up the soil, smelling it, and letting it run through his fingers. "Someday you'll make a dandy farmer," Israel would tell him.

Clara enjoyed working with Mama. She liked the cooking and cleaning. She got a lot of satisfaction helping Mama with the washing and folding of the clothes and putting them in drawers. She was learning to iron, but most of all she enjoyed working in the garden. Somehow she felt the presence of God more strongly outside under the sun, feeling the breeze on her cheeks and looking at the fields beyond and the heavens above.

The children enjoyed the summer that year as much as usual. In their free time they ran barefoot in the fields, climbed the trees, swam and frolicked in the stream and followed it, never finding where it began.

That fall the children went off to school as usual. The weather stayed nice, and Clara enjoyed the fall with its noises, smells and sounds as much as always.

They were planning for the holidays and the coming baby. By the middle of October the weather turned unseasonably cold. The ground froze, and the strong wind blew. The little house whistled with the strong wind coming through wherever it could find a crack. Israel had laid up a large amount of wood, judiciously saving it, not knowing what was coming.

One morning as the children readied themselves for school, Clara happened to glance at Mama. *She isn't acting quite herself this morning,* Clara thought to herself. "Mama," she said, "it's almost time for the new baby. Are you sure I can't stay home and help you with Rosemond this morning?"

"No darling, Aunt Genie will be here by mid-day and I don't want you to get behind in your school work. I'll get Rosemond busy helping me around here. Then I'll be fine. You just take care of your brothers for me."

Off they trudged to school. Mrs. Burgess had the little potbellied stove fairly dancing with a sizzling hot, snapping, roaring fire.

"Good morning children," she said as they filed in and took their seats. "My, isn't it cold and damp? I thought I would take the chill out of the air today with a nice fire."

After Bible reading, prayer, and the Pledge of Allegiance, Mrs. Burgess picked up a copy of *Uncle Tom's Cabin* and continued reading where they had left off the last time. Clara felt very cozy and nearly forgot her troubles in the pleasant schoolroom, with the soothing voice of her teacher. But then the nagging fears kept reappearing.

Clara, Walter, and Doris hurried the children home in the afternoon. The weather was still damp and cold, so no one wanted to linger anyway.

As soon as the children entered the house Clara knew things were different. Mama wasn't in the kitchen to greet them, for one thing. Water was boiling on the stove in the big copper kettle, and then Clara heard muffled sobs coming from upstairs. "The baby," she cried, running for the stairs.

"Just one minute," Aunt Genie ordered, standing there as a barrier to block the stairs. "The doctor and Mrs. Snow are with your mother now so she's in good hands. Children, put your lunch pails on the drain board, wash your hands, and sit at the table for some Johnny cake and milk."

"Aunt Genie, is the baby here yet?" Forest wanted to know.

"Not yet, but it should be here soon." In the end, the baby did take an incredibly long time. By the children's bedtime the baby still hadn't arrived.

"Daddy, promise me you will let me know when the baby comes," Clara begged, as Daddy kissed her goodnight.

"I will dear, if it isn't too late, but you need to get to sleep and get your rest. Remember tomorrow is a big day. We'll have a new member of the family to meet, so now you go to sleep."

Clara lay there and tried hard, but sleep evaded her. Long after she was in bed she heard her Mother's agonizing cries. Finally exhaustion took over, and she at last fell heavily into sleep.

Opening her eyes to a dim dawn light, Clara heard a strange hush in the house. She could hear muffled sounds coming from her Mother's room. Tiptoeing down the hall, she opened the door and hesitantly stuck her head around it. Before anyone could stop her she ran to the bed and cried, "Oh Mama, the baby! Then, looking at her new sister, she said, "She's so white and still, not like the other babies."

Mrs. Snow came and put her arm around Clara. "Now dear, Mother and your baby sister have had a rough time of it, but they're alright. They just need to rest. Come down and help Aunt Genie and me fix breakfast."

As the days passed, Inez and baby both had a hard time gaining strength. The children were anxious to know what they were going to name their baby sister and to play with her. Aunt Genie tried to keep Rosemond occupied, but of course she was curious to see the baby and also wanted her Mother and no one else.

It was well over a week since the baby girl had arrived and she still had no name. Clara fretted. "I guess she'll always be called 'the baby'," she said flippantly. It didn't look like things would ever return to normal, and Clara was uneasy.

The next Sunday, Uncle Lonz came for Aunt Genie to take her to Caledonia. She had to return for a job waiting for her in Hastings. Mrs. Snow had her own family to look after, too, so she wasn't able to give the Haffs as much time as she would have liked.

Monday morning Inez went out to hang the washing on the line. *My goodness it's cold,* she thought. *I think it will snow before nightfall.* The damp wind felt it was blowing right through her thin coat. On and on she struggled to get the wash on the line.

Finally returning to the kitchen, she fell into her rocker, completely winded from the experience. Israel came in from the barn. "Inez, you should have left the wash for me to hang," he scolded.

"Just let me rest a minute and I'll be fine," she said.

But she wasn't fine. She caught a hard cold, and the next day the baby came down with one. Before Israel could even get the doctor, they both had pneumonia.

Dr. Simons stopped by as often as three times a day, but neither Mother nor baby seemed to get much better.

The rest of the family lay in bed at night listening to the terrible wracking coughs. The baby kept up a whimpering even in her sleep. Finally, Mrs. Snow kept an all-night vigil. Aunt Genie was sent for and was on her way. She dropped her paying job and came immediately to help her favorite niece.

That next Sunday Clara sat in a swing in a pear tree outside the back door. The weather had cleared and warmed. Dr. Simon's horse was once again tied to the post. As Clara was swinging, the blue sky became a brilliant, blue, more so than she had ever seen before. The grass, trees and fields beyond all developed an unreal quality. She felt herself swinging, but also floating, like she had no weight at all.

"Clara" a strong, soothing voice said, "You're going to lose your Mother, but you will be alright, I will take care of you!"

The moment passed, everything returned to normal, and Clara looked around and saw no one. Awed, but concerned, she flew into the house, upstairs to her mother's room. Israel was leaving the darkened room just in time to catch Clara and turn her around. He took Clara aside and told her that her Mama had gone to Heaven. "The baby went with her," he said.

The house was in turmoil later that day as the bodies were prepared and the children consoled. The family walked around as if in a dream. The day of the funeral Daddy carried Rosemond around in a daze. Forgetting himself, he walked into the parlor with her in his arms to the casket where Inez and the baby lay. Rosemond saw her mother and clawed and screamed to get to her. Israel was devastated. Clara watched from the door and came and took her baby sister from Daddy.

Taking Rosemond to the kitchen, Clara sat in Mama's rocker and rocked her baby sister. In a soothing voice she said, "Don't worry, baby sister, I'll take care of you. Mama's not here for you, but I'll take care of you. I'll make sure you are always taken care of." This seemed to comfort Rosemond a little. *But how can she understand when I can't?* Clara wondered. *I will always take care of her, Mama. I promise you that.*

The day of the funeral it was raining. It was a cold, wet rain, but that was how Clara felt inside, so it seemed appropriate. Mother and baby were buried together. Clara's only comfort was that they would go together to Heaven and wouldn't be alone.

Clara was only eleven years old, but she would talk about her Mama for the rest of her life. Her mother's memory never died.

Chapter 10

CLARA WOKE THE NEXT morning feeling very lost. She felt like something terrible was still to happen, that the nightmare was not yet finished. Grief seemed to freeze her thoughts, and she was left with only this deep feeling of apprehension. She rose and quickly dressed herself and Rosemond, then went to get the boys up and ready for the day, not sure of what it would hold. As they came into the kitchen, Aunt Rilla, who had stayed after the funeral, was already fixing breakfast. She seated the children at the table as Israel came in the back door from the morning farm chores. Shedding his coat, he crossed the room to the sink and washed his hands, never uttering a word. He moved as though in a trance. As the children looked at him for some clue as to how to proceed he seemed to look through them as though they were not in the room. Walter voiced their concern, "Daddy what will we do now?"

"We'll just have to carry on now. There's nothing else to do."

"I'll try to take some of the burden off your hands, Israel," Aunt Rilla replied with resolution in her voice. "You children get ready and go off to school," seemed to be her first solution.

So Clara kissed her baby sister goodbye and off they trudged with Forest (who was now in first grade) holding Clara's hand. As Israel stood at the kitchen window and watched them walk away he thought, *They are my children and I have no feeling for them one way or another. Will I ever feel anything again? Lord, where are you? As you have turned away from me, so I will reject you from this day on.* He turned from the window to go through his first day without God.

Returning from school that day the children entered a quiet house. Everything was neat and tidy. The back of the stove had a pot of stew simmering on the burner, but nobody was around. Each one scattered to find some human comfort. Finding no one, they all dragged up the stairs to change out of their school clothes for chores.

As Clara entered her bedroom, which she shared with her baby sister since the time preparations for the new baby were made, something was missing. There was no crib. She looked in the chest of drawers she shared with Rosemond and saw that everything of her sister's was gone! With fear in her heart, Clara ran to find Daddy to give him the news. She felt frantic, thinking Rosemond had been stolen.

She ran and ran until her sides hurt, all the way to the far corner of the cornfield where she found her father shocking corn stocks. "Daddy," she cried out, "someone has taken Rosemond. She's gone her, and all of her things!"

He stopped the horse and took Clara in his arms. He explained that Aunt Rilla had taken Rosemond home. "She'll be better off there. I have the farm to run, and you are in school all day. She needs someone to care for her, and Aunt Rilla loves her so." Clara felt betrayed. God must not care for her. How could He let this happen?

At supper that night, with an empty heart, Daddy prayed, "Thank you for this food, Lord," followed by a long pause, then, "Amen."

They ate the stew Aunt Rilla left on the stove and the bread she left in the breadbox, and the pudding Clara had attempted. After the strained meal Israel and the boys went out to do the evening chores. Clara watched them from the kitchen window, Forest lagging behind, looking forlorn and alone, even though he was with his brothers and father.

With stooped shoulders Clara picked up the dishes from the table and washed them. She then picked up the big kettle from the stove and attempted to rinse the dishes with the hot water. *Only two weeks ago Mama did this part. She said that I was too little to handle the scalding hot water*, Clara thought. Was it only that long ago that Mama got sick? It seemed like so long since she had seen her mama. Sometimes to Clara it seemed like a lifetime, at other times only yesterday. She swept up the floor and went to the shed off the kitchen to put the milk the boys had left into the cream separator for the night. She would have to get up at five o'clock in the morning to get the cream taken care of and the butter churned before breakfast before she could help everyone get everyone ready before school. Having finished with everything, she sat down in Mama's rocker and waited. Daddy and the boys came in, and they all sat looking at each other, wondering what to do or say next. Walter took care of that. "Daddy, will you read the book mommy was reading to us?"

"Yes, why don't you bring it here?" Israel answered, glad for something, anything to do before it was time for him to escape to the dark cover of his bed. He opened the book at the place where Inez had marked with a crocheted cross and began where she left off. Struggling to swallow the lump in his throat, he read mechanically. Clara's mind wandered as he read. She heard Mama's voice, soft, rhythmically rising and falling with the flow of the story. Mama could read a story with feeling. At last, it was time for bed. The children were sent upstairs to prepare. As they washed and brushed their teeth and got into nightclothes, Clara looked at the clean things Mama had done up and thought, *I will never get all the things Mama did done and still be in school all day. What will we do?*

Once they were all ready for bed, she ushered them to Walter's bed, and together they said their prayers and went off to their separate beds.

Clara lay in bed and stared in the dark. Sleep would not come. She looked over at the empty space where Rosemond's bed used to be and knew that it was no use to try sleeping. Climbing out of bed, she went softly to the window. The sky was full of stars.

Mama, are you up there? Can you see me? The Bible says, "There will be no more sadness." Are you happy mama? I wish that I could be there with you.

She then heard an audible voice, "Clara." Again, "Clara." Her whole being was filled with unexplainable peace. "Clara, stay there where you are. I have much for you to do."

Standing there in her white nightgown, looking up at the heavens, she felt strangely comforted. She sat there a long time and prayed sincerely to God. Her whole body felt lighter and less lonely. She lay down and covered herself and in a few minutes fell asleep and slept soundly until morning.

Chapter 11

FOR A TIME, FRIENDS and neighbors came in to help with the many chores previously done by Inez which Israel and the children were not capable of doing. Israel was trying to keep up the farm and also be father and mother to his children. The boys were helping on the farm, of course, and Clara tried to fill her mother's shoes, but it was a big job for a little girl indeed! Eventually things fell behind.

John and Ellen stopped by one evening in early December. Israel and the children were just finishing supper. Ellen glanced around at the disorderly kitchen and thought of how mortified Inez would be at the shambles it had become in just six short weeks. Clara followed Ellen's eyes and felt ashamed. She knew she didn't have time to keep it the way her mother always had, but she did wish she could do more.

"Clara, I'll help you with dinner dishes tonight. I know how much easier it is with more hands helping. I miss having a daughter like you to help me," Ellen said as she jumped up and started clearing the dishes.

After dishes Ellen whipped up a pretty "Floating Island" dessert pudding. The children stood there watching the procedure, anticipating the delightful dessert. Turning to Israel, Ellen said, "I'd like come over once in a while and do some of the things you don't have time to do. I know how busy you are with all the responsibilities you have now."

"No," he said, too loudly, "I'll have to learn to manage myself or find my own way out." With resignation and to soften his words, he added, "I can't depend on other people forever." Easing the awkward moment as Ellen poured them coffee, John said, "Israel, do you think seed prices will go up this year?"

"John, I can't even think about farm prices now. All I can do is take what needs doing each day and work my way through it," Israel said, more sharply than he intended.

As they prepared to leave, Ellen turned to Israel and said, "You know Israel, Christmas will be upon us before we know it, and John and I want to invite you and the children over for Christmas dinner."

"Well no," Israel said, "I was thinking of inviting Aunt Genie to come and stay here for a few days at Christmas." He said this to get out of opening the family up to a holiday spent with the memories of pleasant times in the past when Inez was here. *If Aunt Genie is able to come, that will relieve me of some of the tensions of trying to interact all day with the children,* he thought to himself.

Christmas was a dismal affair. They went through all the motions. They had a tree, and Israel purchased small gifts for each of the children. He did his best, even if the things weren't all that appropriate.

They were invited to several homes of family or friends, but Israel wasn't ready to accept any invitation. He felt it would open up feelings too fresh to be tampered with. There would be reminders of the love and joy he and Inez and the children had experienced together with family and friends, which was more than he could expose them to right now. Aunt Genie declined to come visit, explaining she felt she needed to be with Uncle Lonz this year. Israel thought it was probably because she couldn't bear the pain of Inez not being there. Who could blame her? He would like to have escaped, too.

Clara, however, wanted so much to be with the extended family for exactly the same reasons. She wanted to feel the warmth and joy of the love which would be showered on them, wanted what life until now had always been. Subconsciously, she knew this wouldn't make it so, but she wanted to try, to pretend all was well.

And so the family had Christmas. Plenty of food was brought in, and thoughtful people remembered the children with gifts.

Clara tucked the cloth ball she had lovingly made for Rosemond in the back of her drawer in the dresser, along with the handkerchief she had labored over, crocheting lace around the edges for her mother. It was now wrinkled and stained with tears Clara had shed.

Christmas morning dawned bright and beautiful with fresh snow on the ground. Israel had wanted it to storm to match the emotions he was feeling.

They woke up early (not as early as usual) and mechanically opened the gifts. The smaller children seemed happy and enjoyed the gifts, but the morning lagged.

Finally dinner was ready. It even came together okay. Eating was a chore for Clara. She felt like there was a stone in the back of her throat. She tried to swallow the food, but it was hard to get it past that stone.

In the afternoon, dinner was cleared and a blaze was in the fireplace. They sat watching the smaller boys play with their toys. At times Clara even felt glimpses of peace or contentment or some pleasant feeling, but then those feelings would disappear too quickly to latch onto.

Then Israel, Walter, and Francis went out to do the chores. Forest was playing on the floor with two little farm vehicles he received for Christmas. Clara picked up a book she received from Aunt Genie in the mail, and, for the first time since Inez died, was able to get into a novel. Reading about a happy family in a make-believe world helped her forget for a while. She was surprised when her father and brothers came in from the chores. Time had passed so quickly.

That night in bed, using her flashlight, she snuggled up in her blankets and read far into the night, finding comfort in a fantasy world.

Israel, however, lay in his big bed feeling deserted. On the side next to his was a vast emptiness. It seemed only moments before when sweetness and love filled this empty space. He couldn't reconcile the difference, didn't feel he could go on, like he wouldn't go on except for the children. They had lost their mother and three baby sisters, including Rosemond. He couldn't bring them more pain.

Thoughts of Rosemond made him feel guilty. Oh, he could rationalize letting Rilla take her, telling himself that she was better off, but he felt like a coward for letting her take Rosemond off that way. He thought of the look in those sad, deep hazel eyes of Clara's and remembered the pain on her face when she found Rosemond gone. He knew also Inez would not have approved. "But what else could I do?" he said out loud into the darkness.

He tossed and turned until dawn and was glad for another day in which he could forget his struggle and go through the day's endless chores.

For the rest of Clara's vacation from school she found time to be outside sledding with the boys or making snowmen and such. She was finally able to get outside of herself and think of how their mother's death must have felt for the poor little tykes. But whenever possible, she stole away to read and found solace there.

One afternoon, while playing in the snow, Forest lay down to make an angel by flapping his arms and legs. He got up and announced, "Look everyone, I made an angel!"

Clara stood staring at it. Somehow it came alive, lifted itself from the ground and took on such a bright, ethereal quality like she'd never seen before. She thought, *Mama, are you up there with the angels?* She felt her mother speaking to her. *You are going to be okay Clara. You will make it. Little by little, you will make it.* The soothing, melodious voice gave her courage. All of a sudden she felt strong, like she could go on.

The moment passed as Francis stared at her. He had been trying to say something to her. That moment was enough to give Clara courage!

As the children trudged back to school, things went on as usual, pretty much the same on the outside. Members of the Haff family were learning to go on without Inez,t some would learn, others would not.

Chapter 12

ISRAEL SAT BEFORE THE fire, chewing on his pipe. The Free Methodist magazine was before him on his crossed knee.

The younger boys had been put to bed, but Clara and Francis were allowed to stay up a little longer. The children were back in school now, but Forest was having so much trouble with his studies. He just couldn't seem to concentrate. It wasn't easy for the rest of them, either, but he was still so little and frail to have lost his mother. He was only seven years old.

Supper had been a disaster. Besides the meal being served late, Clara had scorched the potatoes, Walter spilled his milk, and there was no butter for the biscuits, since Clara had run out of time that morning to churn it. Things were getting further behind and couldn't seem to get caught up.

Israel finally cleared his throat and spoke. "I'm thinking maybe the thing to do would be to hire a housekeeper."

"Can we afford one?" Clara wanted to know.

"Would it be someone we don't know?" Frances asked.

"Well, here's an advertisement for someone willing to come for $1.75 a week plus board. It does seem too good to be true, but maybe we should give her a try. Things really can't get much worse around here." Clara cringed, feeling that if she could do more to help this wouldn't be necessary.

That night in bed Clara thought, *Well maybe it will work out better. Maybe a woman is what the boys need right now ... It would be good not to try to keep up with all this work almost by myself. My own school work is falling behind, and besides, Daddy would have less to worry about that way.*

And so even though none of them were excited about it, they all generally agreed that maybe it would work. Only Forest looked a little afraid and apprehensive, but with everyone's assurances he seemed accepting. And so the letter was written.

Everyone waited expectedly for the woman to get here who would put some sense of order back in their lives.

Clara lay in bed at night and, even though she was a little apprehensive, still she began to imagine a woman with bright blue, caring, twinkling eyes. One who would have an understanding of just what they were going through. This woman would quickly get the kitchen back in order. She would bake cookies for the boys, encourage Father, and somehow put life back into this lifeless family. Maybe they would even be able to bring darling Rosemond home again.

The whole family had a certain amount of excitement that Sunday afternoon as they waited for the new housekeeper to arrive. The boys were scrubbed to the point of red cheeks and shiny noses, and their hair was plastered down. They all had clean and ironed clothes (as well as Clara could possibly manage with the experience she had of ironing). She looked at the burned spot on her forearm and pulled down her sleeves as far as she could.

Finally, they heard wagon wheels approaching from the street. The smaller boys went to the window.

"This can't be her. This woman has a group of kids with her," Walter said.

Having heard that, Father no longer resisted and went to the window also. He took one look, and they all trouped outside.

Israel went to the wagon, which by now had arrived at the back door. "Can I help you?" he asked.

"This is the Israel Haff farm, isn't it?" the woman asked. Israel nodded.

"Well I'm the housekeeper you sent for in answer to the advertisement in the Free Methodist Magazine."

"But you didn't mention the children in your letter. Are they all yours?"

"Oh yes, but they aren't any trouble. We'll just double up in the bedroom I asked for, and we'll be just fine." She said this as lightheartedly as the sour-looking woman could.

"Well, I don't know," Israel said as he scratched his head. "Maybe we'll try it for a while." *It can't get much worse around here,* thought.

They all went into the house, but Clara lagged behind. Her dreams were on shaky ground.

Later that afternoon a terrible racket could be heard upstairs with crashing and banging as the housekeeper's boys vied for the best cot to sleep on.

Dora, the new housekeeper, was in the kitchen fixing dinner at the time. "I'll settle those kids," she said, heading upstairs.

A few minutes later, down she came. "Clara, you don't mind sharing your room with Hulda, do you? You have so much room, and she'll only take up a little corner!"

Clara shrugged her shoulders and smiled in frustration. What else could she do? She did have the room, but she liked her privacy and had the extra space reserved for Rosemond.

That night in bed, Hulda, almost a year older than Clara, talked and talked until Clara grew sleepy. She snuggled down in bed and turned over. *So far,* she thought, *nothing is turning out as I planned. I don't think I like Hulda, and I didn't even have time to read in bed.* She sighed.

The next day all ten children were sent off to school. That didn't go well, either. The new boys were so mischievous the teacher looked frazzled by the end of the day. Hubert, the oldest, had to stand in the corner half the afternoon for being so disruptive. Clara was so embarrassed she sank down in her chair and pretended she didn't know them. The Haff children were always well behaved.

When the children got home, the wonderful smell of cookies filled the kitchen as they entered. However, there was so much quarreling Clara left the room and went to her bedroom to catch up on her reading. After supper that night, Clara did the dishes by herself. Hulda had a bad headache just at the right time. Homework at the kitchen table was no better. *How could anyone study with so much commotion?* Clara thought to herself.

The next morning snow was piled so high there would be no school. If there were any thoughts of sending the newcomers away, they quickly disappeared, for there would be days before the roads could be traveled.

Chapter 13

THE CLOSE LIVING GOT on everyone's nerves, but the deep snow did eventually dwindle, and now the kids were back in school. It didn't look like Dora and her wild children would be going away soon. Even though the house was in a constant state of uproar, Israel was coming to depend on Dora more and more. She was a decent housekeeper and cook, and it lightened his load considerably. He just spent more time out in the barn and fields. This way he didn't have to face what was happening to his household.

Forest was still the baby with Rosemond gone, and Dora treated him that way. This was just what he most needed at this time and so he took to her. Francis and Walter were able to somewhat control their situation with Dora's kids with threats and promises. There was certainly enough happening at school with that rowdy bunch to bribe them. Clara was the one who felt the brunt of the burden as she seemed to be at the mercy of both Dora and Hulda.

Today, however, Clara opened her eyes to a beautiful, clear morning with her spirits soaring. Aunt Genie had planned an all-day shopping trip with Clara in Grand Rapids. Uncle Lonz had delivered Aunt Genie the afternoon before, and Daddy would be driving the two of them to Middleville to catch the train within the hour.

Clara crept from bed and quietly washed and dressed so she wouldn't take any chances on waking Hulda. She wasn't invited to go along, but

Clara didn't want her conniving to go with them at the last minute, either. She tiptoed down the stairs.

The three travelers ate a quick breakfast of oatmeal. "Clara, I'll need you to set the table for the rest of the family before you go," Dora quibbled.

"Hulda can do that for once," Aunt Genie snipped. Nothing was said. Not even Dora crossed Aunt Genie.

The train ride was so enjoyable. This was the first time since Mama's death Clara had been on a train. Clara remembered many times going with Mama to Grand Rapids on the train to buy fabric to make clothes for her family. As the train went clickety-clack down the tracks, Clara sat, remembering those times. She seemed carried back in time. She could almost smell Mama's lilac toilet water and the fresh clean scent Mama always had. She felt a contentment she hadn't experienced since Mama's illness.

Too soon the train ride was over, and they stepped off the train to the smell of horses with buggies waiting to carry them to the business district.

Time passed so quickly just looking at everything. They went to the local tearoom for a light lunch, and Clara felt that she had been transported to the lap of luxury. She noticed Aunt Genie looking at her shabby coat and felt ashamed. After lunch they walked to a department store.

"Clara," Aunt Genie said, "I would like to buy you a decent coat. Do you think you can take good care of it so it will last through high school?"

"Oh Aunt Genie, I couldn't let you do that!" Clara couldn't believe she heard her aunt right. Aunt Genie never spent a dime she didn't have to; her reputation was well-known.

"I feel I owe it to your mother. She was always so generous with me, so don't argue!" Clara didn't.

They shopped for just the right coat. They both chose a lovely deep green one with a rabbit fur collar. Clara held her breath as Aunt Genie considered it. "It's such a nice color on you, and the wool is good quality." To the clerk she said, "It's much too expensive. If you will knock off two dollars I will take it," but the woman looked doubtful. This tiny little woman stood there and bargained with the big sales lady until they struck up a bargain she liked. The coat was finally purchased, and Aunt Genie let Clara wear it home. It seemed to Clara that Aunt Genie held her head up a little higher after that.

All too soon the day passed, and on the train ride back Clara sat deep in thought. *This was such a wonderful day,* she thought, *that pesky family can do as they please! I'll just transplant myself back to this day and feel happy all over again.*

When she walked in the door with her coat on, she noticed Hulda's eyes turn green with envy. Clara hoped she wouldn't cause any trouble over it. She really didn't want Hulda to resent her.

Later, she overheard Dora talking to Hulda. "The coat is much too rich for the likes of her," Dora was saying, "I'm sure she won't appreciate it or take good care of it."

As the days and weeks went by, Clara noticed when she wore the coat Hulda and Dora looked with jealousy at it. As much as she enjoyed wearing such a fine coat she began to feel a little self-conscious about it.

Each time she took it off, she hung it carefully in the closet so the hangers were just at the seams like Aunt Genie had instructed her.

Spring came early that year, and it helped to have the large household spread outdoors. Then summer came and was also fairly tolerable, but it was moving quickly. Dora made herself indispensable to Israel, who seemed to have lost every bit of drive he possessed. Life seemed to have given him too many blows for him to recover.

One evening Clara sat on the front porch, rocking in the cool of the day and thinking about the upcoming school year. Israel and Dora were in the front room talking. As they did, Dora's voice rose. "Israel,

I'm not getting any younger, and I don't intend to sit here on your farm being your housekeeper into my old age. If we don't get married I'll just pack up and leave."

"Dora, don't get excited. I just have to get used to the idea. I have to think it through."

"This is nothing new. We've talked about it before. If you can't make up your mind, I'll just pack up and I'll leave."

"Well I suppose we might as well get married. I certainly don't know how we would manage without you, and that would give us more bedroom space."

Clara turned cold inside in spite of the warm evening. *So that's what she's been up to with making all of Daddy's favorite dishes and sweet-talking him like she has been,* Clara thought. *How can I possibly stand it?* She sat rocking and thinking 'til long after dark.

Chapter 14

ISRAEL AND DORA DID get married that summer, less than a year after Inez died. Clara was twelve years old. Dora stopped sweet-talking Israel and resorted to orders to get what she wanted. Israel became more and more withdrawn and sulky. His painting was completely set aside. Friends and relatives came around less and less. Clara knew it was because Daddy was so inhospitable, and Dora was downright unfriendly to them.

She didn't blame them for not coming around. Sometimes she didn't feel like being there, either. Then she felt guilty for feeling that way because of her brothers. *What would Mama think?*

That summer was a pretty good year for crops. The rain came when it was needed, and the sunshine was plentiful.

Clara sat down by the creek one day toward the end of summer in the low branch of a stately old oak tree. She liked to come here and seemed to be spending more and more time here whenever she could get away. The water ran merrily along, singing and gurgling and sparkling. *It's so peaceful and beautiful,* she thought, *I should be feeling good but I am feeling so hopeless. Mother, why did you leave us now? This summer would have been so wonderful with you still around. The crops and weather are perfect! When you were here the farm never produced this well. Why now? It just seems like it's all wasted with Daddy so down, and so much is wrong with the people in our house. No one seems happy. Without you everything is wrong!* Lately Clara felt very uneasy about the way in which Dora's boys looked at her. It was as if they were looking at her with her clothes off. She also didn't like the way they touched her at times. She felt very vulnerable and uncomfortable but wasn't sure why. At that point she sighed and told herself maybe when school started next week things would be different. She glanced up and saw Hulda coming down the hill.

"Clara, Mama needs you to come and help with supper. You should have been up there helping with the washing. Now she's all tuckered out."

Clara felt there was no way to escape this miserable situation. *How can I endure it?* she wondered to herself as she dragged up the hill.

School did start the next week, and it seemed to help with the tensions in the household as things settled into a routine.

Clara loved school and was able to spend much of her time in her room at home doing homework.

She had quite a walk to the high school in Caledonia, but she didn't mind. It was a good transitional time between home and school. Besides, she met Effie Dickerson that fall. Effie lived about halfway between Clara's home and school. They walked together and were becoming fast friends. Some of the boys walked behind and teased them. One day Effie had on a beautiful yellow blouse, which was striking with her black curly hair. Her skirt was red and pleated at the hips.

"Red and yellow catch a fellow," one of the boys shouted.

"Don't mind him," Clara whispered. "I think he likes you." Clara thought Effie was beautiful and wished her own clothes weren't quite so shabby. She also wished she had gotten more sewing lessons from Mama. *Dora probably wouldn't let me have money for fabric anyway,* Clara thought. *Pretty soon I'll be able to wear my coat. That will cover my old clothes.*

One morning she woke up to a cold bedroom. She jumped up and quickly washed at the commode and dressed. She then ran to the kitchen to warm by the fire.

Dora was fixing breakfast, "Where have you been?" she asked. Clara didn't answer. She was so tired of the same question every morning. Instead, she started setting the table.

When the children were all down, and Daddy and the boys came in from the barn, they had breakfast and Clara and Hulda did the dishes.

"Clara, you are going to be late," Dora yelled. Hulda stood there with a smug, satisfied look on her face.

Clara ran to the closet to get her coat, excited by the prospect of wearing it. She quickly looked through the coats, and her new one was missing. Fear gripped her heart.

"Has anyone seen my new coat?" she asked.

"No we haven't. I can't help it if you don't take care of your things. This is what you get!" Dora chided.

"I hung it right here in this closet," Clara said with a sinking feeling in the pit of her stomach.

"Wear your old coat," Dora yelled. "It's good enough for someone who doesn't take care of her clothes."

Clara looked at Daddy, and he looked away.

Dejectedly, Clara put on her old, threadbare coat that was too small. She slipped out of the house and walked down the driveway and up the road to meet Effie.

"What's the matter Clara?" Effie asked. "You look like you've lost your best friend, and you haven't, because I am your best friend, aren't I?"

Clara explained what happened and everything just came tumbling out. Effie felt so bad for her that she didn't know what to say. "Listen, why don't you come home with me after school and talk with my mother about it? She'll know what to do."

Clara agreed to that, not knowing what else she could do. Maybe Effie's mother could think of something.

The Dickerson kitchen was warm and friendly, like Clara's used to be. Effie's mother had just finished baking good-smelling cookies. She invited the girls to sit down and have some with milk. She also sat down at the cheery kitchen table with a cup of tea.

"Clara, how are you getting along now that your father's remarried?"

It doesn't seem possible Inez has been gone a year already. I miss her at the missionary meetings. She was so talented with quilts and such."

"Mother, this is why I invited Clara home." Effie said. "She's not getting along well at home, and I thought she might talk to you."

"Clara, dear, why don't you tell me all about it? I do want to help if I can."

For about an hour Clara poured out her heart to this kind, sincere woman who asked questions and made sounds of knowing and sympathy from time to time.

"Clara, I'm so sorry to hear things are going this way. You've been through so much already. I have to admit that I'm not surprised. I've been hearing rumors, but so hoped they weren't true. I do want to help you, but first I need some time to pray about it. I do have an idea, but I want to check it out. Why don't you go home now and try not to aggravate Dora any further or be alone with those boys. Come back on Monday, and we'll talk some more."

Chapter 15

SATURDAY MORNING PROVED TO be as hectic as ever. Things should have gone better with three capable women living in the house. However, Hulda dragged her feet at every chore she was expected to do. She would mope around with the dust cloth and give the furniture a swipe. After a minute or two Dora would take the cloth from her hand and put some elbow grease into it, but Clara was then the one assigned to the job Dora had been doing. This went on until well after lunchtime.

"Ma, I promised Elsie I would be over shortly after lunch to do homework together with her," Hulda whined.

"Well sweep the kitchen floor before you go, and Clara can mop it."

This was news to Clara, and she resented it. She vowed to try once again to talk to Father when her work was done.

After she mopped the kitchen floor (which she had to sweep over again to get the dust bunnies from under the furniture), she ran out to the field where Israel was busy harvesting the last of the corn. She waited with cold water from the well until he slowed the horses and came over, grateful for the water.

"Daddy, I just can't stand much more of Hulda's laziness and Dora babying her. She gets her way on everything, and I end up doing twice the work."

"Well Clara, I know it's an adjustment on everyone, but just give it time," which was what he always said when she complained to him. Clara felt so helpless and frustrated she decided to tell him of her other worry, too. Dora's boys had been touching her in ways that made her feel uncomfortable. They ogled her up and down when they thought no one was looking. When she told her father, he seemed surprised and embarrassed and mumbled something about speaking to them.

Somehow the weekend passed. On Monday morning on the way to school, Effie said her mother had definitely been working on a plan and wanted Clara to stop by on her way home from school.

Excited by the idea that Effie's mother had something in mind, Clara had a hard time keeping her mind on her school work that day. As a result the day dragged on.

After school that day the girls walked home in the cold, brisk air. The holidays were coming upon them, a dismal thought for Clara. She tried not to think about it at all.

As Effie opened the back door from the shed into the bright kitchen a feeling of warmth and peace came upon Clara. She could almost imagine it was her kitchen when her mother was alive.

The girls sat at the table eating cookies and drinking hot chocolate while Mrs. Dickerson was busy at the stove, beginning preparations for supper.

She fixed herself some tea and sat down.

"Clara, the Conners, who live in the farm about a mile past the church, are in need of help running the farm. They are getting older and can't get around as well as they used to.

They are looking for live-in help and would pay a few dollars besides. If you wanted to try it for a while, at least it would get you out of a bad situation and give you money for clothes and such."

"I have never thought of leaving home. I don't know what Daddy would say," Clara replied. The thought came to her mind that she would be leaving her brothers there without her protection.

"Why don't you go home and discuss it with your father," Effie's mother suggested.

After supper and chores, Israel was out in the barn milking. Clara slipped her coat on and ran to the barn.

"Daddy," she said when she found him, "the Conners need someone to help them with chores now that they are getting older. I thought I might go talk to them about it."

Israel thought a minute and said, "That might be a good idea to get you out of the house more often. It might prove to be better all around."

"Well they were thinking of someone living with them for room and board, and they would be able to pay a little, too. I could use that money for clothes."

Daddy looked pained. "Clara, I hate it to go this way, but maybe it's for the best, with Dora's brood, that is, if you take the job. It's not far from here, and we could still see each other often. The holidays are coming, so you'll be over there then when Dora's boys are home, and it will be a shorter walk to school for you, too. Let's go talk to them Saturday morning."

So it was agreed upon.

Israel did take Clara over to see the Conners that Saturday morning. Mrs. Conner invited them into her cheerless kitchen where she served tea.

The woman wore a long gray plain dress. Her hair was pulled back into a severe bun. She was the saddest-looking woman Clara had ever seen. Reading more into her face than Clara even knew gave them an immediate connection.

Mr. Conner came in from the garden toting some late fall vegetables and laid them on the sink board. He turned and sized Clara up. "Well you're awfully little. Do you think you could help 'Mama' in the house and still be able to help me some on the farm?"

Daddy spoke up then and said, "Oh, don't let her size fool you. She's a good worker and very dependable."

"I would like to try," Clara said. "I think I could be help here. It's closer to the school, and that would give me more time."

The four of them agreed over a cup of tea. It was arranged that Daddy would bring Clara and her things over Monday after school.

When Dora heard, she thought it was a good idea also. Only she was selfishly looking at the money coming to her. Israel for once put his foot down and said "No, that little bit of money will be for Clara to buy decent clothes and books for school."

"Well, she can come back on Saturday morning and help with the cleaning," Dora determined.

"No, and I don't want to hear another word about it," Israel said on his way out the door to the barn.

Chapter 16

MONDAY AFTER SCHOOL, ISRAEL loaded the buggy with Clara's meager belongings, and together they rode over to the Conner's. It was a quiet ride. They each sat reflecting on the past and what might have been.

Israel thought of all of the plans he and Inez had for Clara when she was born. So much love would be poured on her, and they would give her opportunities neither of them had. Now it seemed everything was falling down at his feet. It was a struggle just to go on. He wondered where it could possibly end up. What could he give their children now? Their firstborn was leaving home under stressful circumstances, at a tender age, working hard just to survive. *What have I done?* he thought. *I couldn't have continued the way things were going. I couldn't find paid help. Oh, Inez, maybe I shouldn't have married Dora, but then what would I have done? I couldn't have found help that I that I could afford. I'm just sorry this big brood came into our lives.*

"You never consulted me, Israel," a voice from nowhere seemed to say. Startled, he came to the present. No one was around. It wasn't Clara's voice. *I've rejected God so why should he speak to me?* Israel thought. *He wasn't there when Inez died, so why would he be there now?* He shook his head as if to clear it, shrugged his shoulders, and looked at Clara, wondering her thoughts, poor girl.

Clara rode along with a lump in her throat. *Why do I feel so bad about leaving?* she was thinking. *Home just isn't the same as it was when Mama was there. At home, I just don't like leaving the boys and Daddy. Its so hard to accept that things will never be the same with Mama gone.*

It seems like the heart is gone from us. I don't know what will happen to family, or what's left of it.

So it was with a sense of doom that father and daughter arrived at the Conners'.

Clara's things were carried up to the room she was to occupy. The room seemed stark but convenient. Downstairs again Israel kissed her goodbye and said, "Clara, let me know if you need anything."

"I'll be fine, Daddy, I'm sure," Clara bravely replied.

As she went back upstairs, she quickly put away her things and then went to the kitchen to help Mrs. Conner with supper preparations. She quietly stepped in and worked along this sad, depressed lady. *I feel peaceful here anyway,* she thought. *It does feel good not to have all the uproar of our house all the time.* She then felt badly thinking of her father and brothers still having to put up with it, and what about Rosemond? She probably feels deserted. Clara felt so removed from her baby sister.

"Mrs. Conners" she said, "did you ever have children?" The old lady's face took on such an anguished wistful look that Clara was sorry she asked about it. After what seemed an eternity of awkward silence, Mrs. Conners answered.

"Oh yes", she said hesitantly, looking out the window as if to find this part of her life which the dear old people felt best left alone, as if this part of her had been dried up. "My first-born Albert left home at the age of sixteen over some disagreement or other with his father, and went out west to seek his fortune." She had a dreamy-like look on her face. "He was always so difficult. He had fits of temper, swearing, and carousing. We just couldn't understand him." Her face brightened. "Then there was Alma. Never was a sweeter child. She was such a joy to be around, and she never said a cross word. She had the look of an angel, with blond, curly hair, the bluest eyes I've ever seen, except for her daddy's. She married right out of high school and delivered a baby a year later. Both mother and child died at birth. I still can't believe it. God wouldn't do that. I just don't understand. Listen to me, going on like an old fool. Here comes Seth from the west field. He'll be ready for supper. Check those potatoes, will you?" she said, scurrying around.

"Clara," Mr. Conner said at supper, "we want you to be comfortable here. We haven't had a young person around in quite some time. You'll pardon us if it takes a while to get used to you being here."

"I want to be able to help you both. I really didn't do a lot before Mama left us, but since then I've sure done my share."

"Well, I hope you'll be able to help the Mrs. in here and me some outside. In the morning I'll call you to help me will the chores, and then we'll come in for breakfast, and you can help Mama clean up and then get to school."

After supper dishes and chores with Mr. Conners were finished, Clara went up to her new room and sat at the desk doing homework. She tried hard not to think about home, but her mind kept wandering back.

The boys will be at the kitchen table doing their homework, too, she thought. *Dora's brood will be there, doing their utmost not to do theirs. I hope my brothers can keep up with their studies enough so they can keep from falling behind.*

Her own homework done at last, Clara crawled into bed with her favorite book, *The Girl of the Limberlost*. She reflected on how life seemed so unfair.

The girl of Limberlost's mother was so mean and unloving until it was almost too late. Clara's mother was the most kind, good, loving mother she knew, but wasn't able to stay here with them. How can that happen?

Clara put her book down and blew out the lamp. She buried her head in the pillow and cried herself to sleep, which really didn't take too long since the day had worn her out so.

"Clara, it's time to get up and get at the chores to be finished in time for breakfast." It took a minute to realize where she was and that there had been a knock on her door.

She looked out the window and saw that it was pitch dark. Her clock on the desk said 4:30. She jumped out of bed and hit the cold floor. As she did so the shock of it brought her quickly awake. She hurriedly washed and dressed. She did not want to be late on her first day of work.

As she entered the barn she felt the warmth. The cattle mewed softly as Clara and Mr. Conner came in. She arranged herself at the first cow in the line Mr. Conner had given her to milk. "Flossy" was the name on a board overhead. She looked at Clara with soft brown eyes and long lashes as if to say "Good morning, I'm glad you're here." The cow nudged Clara with her soft nose as she came into the stall to relieve her of a full udder of milk. This good-natured cow soon became a favorite of Clara's. The smell of milk and fresh hay Mr. Conner tossed into the manger gave her a peaceful feeling.

Then there was the assortment of kittens and cats all wanting a squirt of milk, which she willingly gave them, adding to the contentment she felt.

"Clara, don't waste too much time on the cats, or you'll miss your hot breakfast" Mr. Conner said with an underlying tone of kindness.

As they started back to the house for breakfast the sun was just peeking over the horizon. Clara felt the warmth of it and was glad. Then, thinking of last night reminded her of how dreary and depressing it seemed here, but now she thought, *I might really like it here. The Conners seem so lonely and sad, but I think they just miss their children. They are good people and I really hope my being here will make them happier.* Her feeling didn't last long as she thought of her father and brothers and Rosemond and how it was for them. She pushed down those feelings as she poured the milk into the cream separator in the back shed.

They all had a nice warm breakfast, and then she hurried through the rest of her duties and ran down the driveway to catch up with Effie to walk to school.

Chapter 17

A s CLARA TOOK OFF her coat after school, Mrs. Conner watched as she hung it up on the peg at the back door. "Clara, why don't you come upstairs with me? I have something to show you." At the top of the stairs, Mrs. Conner opened a door, and, taking Clara by the arm, she ushered her into a room Clara hadn't been before. "This is Alma's room," she simply said.

Stepping into the room, the afternoon sun shined through the window, revealing a neat tidy room. The bed was made without a wrinkle with a pretty yellow ruffled bedspread. The dresser and commode shone with a recent polishing. Not a dust mite could be seen in the air or any dust on the floor. Pretty rag rugs covered a spotlessly clean, polished floor.

As the old woman opened a chest, a tear trickled down her cheek. She lovingly sorted through and found a fine red wool coat. "Here, try this on," she said.

"Oh no, I couldn't. This must have been Alma's, wasn't it?" Clara said, shrinking back.

"I want you to have it if it fits. It's not doing anyone any good shut up in this chest! You'd be doing me a favor wearing it. Here, let's see if it fits," Mrs. Conner said, as she slipped it on a hesitant Clara.

"Your coat's getting pretty small for you," she stated as Clara stood there feeling the soft lining. Mrs. 'C' buttoned it for her.

"Well, this one is a little large, but I imagine you'll grow into it before long. I don't want to hear any more about it!"

As Clara put the new coat on for school the next day, she held her head just a little higher. With a surprised look Mr. Conner glanced at his wife. There was an unspoken question on his face. His wife just gave him a knowing, pleased look.

"Well Clara if you don't look dapper in that coat. That red just makes those sharp hazel eyes of yours light up," he said.

Near the end of the week Clara decided she would ask if she might meet the boys at school and walk home with them on Friday.

She arrived as the children were leaving the schoolyard. Her brothers came running to meet her.

"Clara, how is it at the Conners'? Are they treating you alright?" Francis wanted to know.

"Clara, where did you get your new coat?" Walter asked with admiration.

"I have a new puppy," Forest said proudly. They all started talking at once sharing all the news.

"There was a letter from Aunt Rilla, and they are bringing Rosemond for a visit," said Forest importantly.

"When are they coming?" Clara asked.

"Next Sunday. They'll be here in time for dinner. Can you come over then, Clara?"

"I'll find a way somehow," she replied. The visit with her brothers was short because they all had chores to get home to.

The rest of the week went by so slowly. On Saturday, besides the outdoor chores, Clara and Mrs. Conners cleaned and baked all day, and that night Clara fell into a sound sleep and slept until about 3:00 in the morning. She then awoke and became so excited that she was unable to get back to sleep. She thought of how Rosemond must look now. Was her hair long? Was it still curly? Would she know the family? She was so little when she left. It had been over two years since Clara last saw her.

Finally it was time to get up and help Mr. Conners with the milking. The morning dragged. It was arranged that she would go home with her family after church. Dora and Hulda had stayed home to fix Sunday dinner.

Clara walked into the house through the kitchen door, and Hulda greeted her by nudging her shoulder and telling her how hard Hulda had had to work since Clara left.

Clara hung her coat on a kitchen peg and watched it like a hawk. If she had thought of it earlier she would have worn her old one.

"My, that's a pretty coat, Clara. Where did you get it?" Dora wanted to know.

When Clara told her she just said, "Well take care of this one!"

At last the time came for the buggy to arrive. The children stood at the window and watched the buggy drive into the driveway. Clara looked, and there was her darling Rosemond.

She was carried into the house and all the children crowded around her, which made her bashful. She didn't seem to know them. She looked like a different little girl. She had grown quite chubby, and as the afternoon went on, seemed quite spoiled. By the time the Conners picked Clara up, she felt so disheartened.

"How did your afternoon go, Clara?" Mrs. Conners wanted to know.

"Oh Mrs. Conners, things have changed so much. Rosemond is so different. I just feel so bad," she said as she started to cry.

"There, there my dear, I know it's hard, but it will get better as time goes by," she said, putting an arm around Clara and covering her with a blanket.

That night in bed she told Mother all about it. *Mama, I promise you I won't let Rosemond forget us. I'll write her letters reminding her of us, and when I'm older I will go see her and get to know her. I'll never let her forget us.*

The winter wore on, and the holidays seemed pretty dismal. Clara saw her family, but it was all so difficult. They would never be the same again. However, she still went to visit when she could. She didn't want to ever lose touch with them. She wanted them to remember all the love they once had, and so she would keep reminding them.

The Conners found it easier just to ignore the holidays. They had not celebrated since their children were lost to them. Clara found this easier than the state of mind her family was in, and it suited her frame of mind. There was a totally different atmosphere in the Haff household at Christmas now.

I wish Mama was here, she thought. She gathered her brothers in the barn when she was there for the holidays and talked about the happy past they all shared together. And so the heritage of story-telling continued.

Clara Graduating College

Clara, Baby Rosemond, and Walter

Clara, Francis, Forrest, Walter, and Rosemond Haff

Francis, Clara, Walther, Foresst, and Baby Rosemund Haff

Grandmother Martha Jensen

Israel and Inez Haff

Peter Christian Jensen in Danish Army Uniform

Chapter 18

CLARA CAME TO LOVE the Conners and boarded there for several years. More and more, she took over one chore or another that Mrs. Conners had been doing. The dear woman had to rest more and more often now. It became so that Clara worked from the time she got home from school until bedtime. This made it difficult for her to get her homework done. She sometimes worked late into the night to get it accomplished. On more than one occasion, she found herself sleeping with her head on her desk in the morning. She was conscientious about her grades and didn't want to fall behind.

During the spring when she was fourteen, she came in from school one day to find Mrs. Conners on the floor. Dropping her books on the kitchen table, she knelt on the floor beside her. *Please, dear Lord, don't let her die*, she prayed. "Mrs. Conners, please answer me," she said, shaking the woman gently. But there was no response.

Rushing to the sink, Clara wet a wash cloth in a clean bucket of water and kneeled to put it on Mrs. Conners' forehead. Mrs. Conners opened her eyes, and they rolled back in her head. "Mrs. Conners, can you hear me?"

Mrs. Conners struggled up and then suddenly laid back down. "Oh, the pain in my chest,! It's so awful." She opened her pale eyes and focused on Clara. "What happened?"

"You must have passed out, Mrs. C. Stay here, and I'll run and get Mr. Conners. Don't move! Just lie there and rest. I'll be right back." She ran to the end of the field where Mr. Conners was cultivating and flagged him down.

As she told him what had happened he unhitched the horses from the machine and hurried them to the pasture. "Go back inside and stay with her. I'll be right there."

Minutes later, Mr. Conners rushed into the house and saw his wife lying on the floor. He quickly took Clara's place. "Elsa, it's me darling," he said kneeling by her side. "I'll get the doctor. Don't move. Just stay there and rest," he said, putting a pillow under her head. "Clara, stay here with her and I'll be back as soon as I can." With that, he was gone.

Clara sat on the floor beside this precious old woman and tenderly encouraged her. "Don't die, Mrs. Conners. We need you," she said through tear-stained eyes, giving the woman loving strokes at the same time. She took the afghan from the back of the kitchen rocker and gently covered Mrs. Conners. Clara stayed with her as the afternoon sun moved away.

The doctor arrived, and, with Mr. Conners, lifted her to bed. After a thorough examination Dr. Simons sat the two of them down.

"It appears to be her heart. There are marks on her chest where she's been grabbing it. I think it's been going on for some time."

"What can we do for her?" asked Clara.

"I'll leave some pills she should take when she feels a spell coming on. She'll need plenty of rest for a while."

"School's almost out for the summer, so I'm sure I can do the housework and care for her, too," Clara said eagerly. "I'll do my best at least."

They managed until school was out with friends and neighbors coming in to help. Then Clara took over all summer long doing the cooking and cleaning and nursing, still finding time to help with the farm chores.

Dr. Simons came to visit one morning to see how things were going. He came out of the bedroom after examining the patient and pronounced her significantly better. "Clara, our patient seems to be coming along just fine, but you, young lady, are looking terribly thin and worn!"

"Well, I am working hard, but she should be able to do some of the work soon, shouldn't she?"

She can start doing a little at a time, but Clara, don't overdo it. Let some things go. We don't want you getting sick, too."

I'll try, doctor. I just see so much that needs doing," Clara said with a sigh.

"I mean it, Clara! You never have been strong, and you can't let this job kill you, you know. I know the Conners are happier now that you're here, so if things aren't prefect don't worry about it."

By the end of the summer Mrs. Conners was feeling much stronger and was doing much of the work herself so Clara felt comfortable going back to school.

Effie and Clara walked together to school once again. "Clara, it's so good to see you. I've missed you this summer. You've been so busy with the Conners."

"I know, Effie, I've missed you, too. I feel so good just being a kid again and going off to school. I won't even mind the homework Mrs. Parker gives us. I do worry about Mr. Conner though. The heavy farm work seems to leave him tuckered out."

Clara spent the holidays with her family but made sure to celebrate with the Conners, too. They attended the church services on Christmas Eve and then drove over the crystal snow in the cutter to drop Clara off at her father's house. The night was perfect. The snow sparkled with the full moon smiling down. The stars seemed low over the earth. *Is this how it was the night of Jesus' birth?* Clara wondered. *Mama, are you up there with the stars? I feel you so close to me. I can almost smell your lilac toilet water. I know you're watching over me. How am I doing, Mama? I want you to be proud of me. I'm older now, almost fifteen. Do you like the way I'm growing up?* Clara felt an overwhelming sense of peace, like she really had communicated with her mother.

She went to bed that night knowing she would never be alone. Her mother would always be with her.

Chapter 19

As Clara and Effie walked home from school through the fields, their spirits soared. Light green "fur" dusted the land for miles. The earth smelled fresh and sun soaked it. The girls breathed deeply of the sweet perfume of spring.

Looking up at the newly leafed trees, Clara saw a robin's nest. Mama robin was preparing her nest for the babies she was expecting. Perched next to it was the proud papa-to-be. The mama was chirping orders to him as he stalked the ground below for worms.

Rounding a line of trees planted as windbreakers, they saw in the distance a lump lying at the other end of the field. Hurrying closer, a feeling of dread engulfed Clara. Running now, they came upon Mr. Conners lying beside his cultivator, which had fallen. Clara stumbled to the ground and cried out to him. He opened his eyes and, breathing hard, mumbled her name.

"Effie, run and get Regal the horse in the barn and take him to get the doctor. I'll stay with Mr. Conners." Without a word, the frightened girl was off to get Regal, the fastest horse

Clara cradled the dear old man's head in her lap. He opened his eyes and, struggling, he breathed out, "Clara, I've loved you like my own daughter! You've been such a dear, sweet child." Then fighting for breath, he said, "I don't think I will make it. Take care of Mrs. Conners. She loves you so, Clara."

"No, Mr. Conners, hang on! The doctor's coming," she cried.

It was too late. His eyes closed, and Clara saw that his face was more peaceful and rested than she had seen it in a long time. She knew she couldn't wish him back. He was in the arms of his heavenly Father. Her heart was broken and hurting for herself. "Oh, what will we do without you? You are our rock," she cried.

A little crowd stood at the open grave as a thin, pale, tired old lady threw a handful of dirt on the box that had just been lowered down with a lifetime of memories in it.

Father came and stood by Clara as the mourners left the grave. Effie's mother had Mrs. Conners in tow. "Clara," she said, "some of the neighbors will come by on Saturday and have a talk with Mrs. Conners on what she should do now. I don't think she has any relations except her son out west someplace, does she?"

"I don't think so. Only me," Clara said in a small voice. And then she said, "Mrs. Conners does get a letter once in awhile from someone."

Clara and Mrs. Conners sat down to breakfast the next morning. Everything was the same. The table was set the same as always. The chores were finished. The same homey smell of bacon and eggs, rich cream for the coffee, and sweet farm butter for the toast filled the room. The sunrise was glorious. The house cat sat lapping cream in a saucer on the floor. There was, however, one glaring exception. A chair was empty, and the place setting was missing.

"Mrs. Conner, a few of your neighbors will be coming tomorrow to help you decide what to do now," Clara said.

"Do? What can I do but go on?"

"Well, we can't run the farm alone. They will help you find a way to manage."

"Yes, I see. Well I suppose it's kind of them to want to help. You go to school Clara. I will clean up here."

Throughout the day Mrs Conners thought about what she would do. *I could find a farm hand to work the land,* she thought. *Clara will*

be leaving and going off to college or finding some young man in a year or two. I don't want her to feel obligated to stay or to come home and find me dead. It's getting so difficult for me to manage around the house, and it's lonely without Seth and Clara during the day. Maybe I'll go live with my niece, Anna. She's there alone, too, since she lost her husband. We'll be good company for each other. We've so much to catch up on.

After a long discussion on Saturday, it was decided the best thing to do was for Mrs. Conners to go live with her niece, Anna.

Clara would stay on until this could all be arranged. The farm was sold to a man from the east. He wanted to bring his family out to the Midwest, he said. New York was getting too crowded. He had six children--three boys and three girls. He went back to collect his family and what belongings they could bring. He bought the house and property as is, with all the livestock, equipment, and furnishings.

Mrs. Conners had written her niece, who had quickly replied that she would love to have her favorite Aunt come and live with her. She was very lonely living by herself.

Clara searched the weekly paper and finally came up with an advertisement that seemed to suit her needs. Daddy was picking her up this morning and taking her for an interview.

At 10:00 sharp his wagon drove up. She kissed Mrs. Conners goodbye and told her she would see her by suppertime. "Don't worry about fixing supper. We'll do that together," she said.

The farm was on the other side of Caledonia. Clara didn't like being so far from her family, but the situation seemed to suit her.

It was a beautiful day for a ride and father and daughter were enjoying each other's company.

At noon they arrived in Caledonia and stopped for lunch at a little teashop, an unheard of expense. "Daddy, what will Dora say?" Clara wanted to know.

"About what" He looked at her with pretended innocence.

"Daddy you know about the about what, about this lunch."

"Oh that, well I don't intend to tell her. There's no reason to, and you won't, either," he said meaningfully.

They both fully enjoyed lunching together and were off again. They arrived at the Smith farm about mid-afternoon. Mrs. Smith welcomed them into a cool, somewhat dark parlor where she had a cool coconut cream pie waiting to served.

They talked awhile about what Clara's responsibilities would be, and it all seemed reasonable.

"When will we meet Mr. Smith?" Israel wanted to know.

"Oh, he's in Grand Rapids buying a part for the tractor. He said for me to do what I wanted about Clara." Looking at Clara she said, "Well, it does seem like it will work out given your experience already. Why don't we give it a try?"

It was all arranged. Mr. Smith would pick up Clara and her belongings on Sunday afternoon next.

Saturday, Clara packed up the things Mrs. Conners would be taking to her niece's house—clothes, pictures and a few items around the house she wanted to take with her. A man was hired to take care of the farm until the new owners arrived. He would take Mrs. Conners to Hastings, where her niece lived.

"Clara I want you to have this cedar chest of Alma's. Seth made it for her the summer she turned sixteen."

Clara looked at the beautiful chest, which had a hand carved picture of the farm on it. It was simply magnificent.

"Oh no, I couldn't, Mrs. Conners. You've already given me so much, and it's so precious to you."

"That's why I want you to have it, Clara girl. You have been so precious to us. You brought both of us to life. Besides, I won't have room for any more than I'm already taking, and I don't want to leave it here."

"In that case, I'll treasure it always and I'll never forget the two of you, ever." Tears welled up in Clara's eyes, and she wasn't able to say more. Mrs. Conners wasn't able to say anything either, so instead they hugged each other and shared a good cry.

The next day they went to church together and Clara said goodbye to her family. The visits would be fewer now. It was so much farther away.

Clara and Mrs. Conners drove home in silence. Both had said everything there was to say. Lunch was a dismal affair. Not much was eaten. They both had lumps in their throats.

Like clockwork, after lunch Mrs. Conners' niece arrived. Mrs. Conners was packed into the wagon, and the woman who had become so dear to Clara was driven away. Clara watched her until she was out of sight. She ran back into the house and threw herself on her bed. The loneliest feeling she had ever felt came over her.

She looked out her window into the familiar maple tree. Beams of light shone down on her, and with them she felt that now-familiar sense of peace. "Clara, I will be will be with you wherever you go," a voice seemed to reassure her.

Did she really hear it, she wondered? The feeling of comfort was overwhelming. She must have heard it.

Chapter 20

THE NEXT DAY, MR. Smith came to collect Clara and her meager belongings.

He was a big man with tanned leather skin, probably from farming. He had a ruddy complexion and sandy-colored hair–what there was of it. His half-closed eyes took sidelong glances at Clara that made her feel uncomfortable.

"You certainly are a slight one. You don't look like you're capable of much work," he said, finally.

"Oh, don't worry about that. I've been doing housework and farm chores since my mother died when I was eleven." There was no response. They both lapsed into an uncomfortable silence for the rest of the ride.

They arrived at the Smith farm at suppertime. Clara's things were carried upstairs to a spare, dark room at the back of the house. She washed her face and hands and brushed her hair, then was called down to supper. A meager amount of food was dished onto her plate. Clara was surprised at the small amount she was served. She ate hungrily, this being her first meal since breakfast. It had been a long, hot ride with no stops. Mr. Smith had given her lukewarm water at midday. Clara couldn't help remembering the tearoom lunch she and her father had shared. She had enjoyed the time spent with her father so much, and now this.

"Clara, you go unpack, and I'll do up the dishes," Mrs. Smith generously said.

"Don't spoil her now. Let her help," said Mr. Smith. There was no argument, Clara helped with the dishes.

Now in her room, Clara put her things away. She placed the chest Mrs. Conners had given her lovingly at the foot of her bed. The room had a chilly and damp feel, even though it was a warm day. She opened the window and let in a deliciously fresh breeze. The warm air flowing through seemed to air the room out a bit. She then gave herself a sponge bath, put on a clean nightgown, and sat down at a little table in front of the window to do her homework.

It was then that the loneliness overtook her. She couldn't help drawing comparisons with her time at the Conners and this place. She didn't see how this drab place could ever be home for her. Also, she didn't know what to think about Mr. Smith. She felt uncomfortable about the leering way he looked at her. Still, Mrs. Smith seemed to take an interest in her. She sure seemed stingy, though. Clara concluded she would give the arrangement time and see what became of it. It wasn't like she had any other place to go.

Clara was awakened at 4:30 in the morning for chores. After helping in the barn, she helped finish breakfast and afterward did the dishes. She then walked the three and a half miles to Caledonia High School. She did, after a while, settle in at the Smith farm. Oh, life never seemed what it was when Mama was alive. She also missed the Conners terribly, but still she told herself, "I will make it workable here."

In August, when it was time to harvest wheat, Clara was expected to rise at 4:30 and help with the barn chores as usual. The barn somehow seemed dismal when she compared it to the Conners' warm, friendly barn. Everything was really very orderly, but there was a cold, austere atmosphere about the place, including Mr. Smith. When it was time to go into the kitchen and help Mrs. Smith with breakfast dishes, Mr. Smith said, "Oh, Clara I want you back out in the field as soon as Mrs. Smith can spare you. I need help with the wagon."

Dashing back out after finishing the dishes, Clara ran to the field where two boys were baling hay. Mr. Smith was driving the horses and told Clara to get up in the wagon to help a third boy pile the hay on. In no time at all, the stacks were higher than she could reach comfortably, and her back was throbbing. She was so relieved to see Mrs. Smith coming down the lane to call them to dinner. They all sat down at the kitchen table, very hungry after a morning of hard work. Clara was surprised to see the meager portions of food put on each plate. She noticed Mr. Smith's plate had twice as much and felt disappointed by it. By the end of harvest, Clara's spirits sagged, and she was bone weary.

However, summer moved into fall, and school resumed. Clara loved school, and her spirits picked up dramatically. All of her old friends and the teacher from last year were there. Autumn was always amazing to her, that such wondrous colors could actually be the death of something. She really didn't mind the long walk to school and home again. The sights and sounds pleased her and the smells lifted her spirits so. The air grew nippy in the mornings, but by afternoon a delicious warmth enveloped her.

Mrs. Smith seemed to like her well enough. She was even teaching Clara to sew. Clara had managed to buy a few things at the Conners', and she also had Alma's clothes that Mrs. Conners had insisted she have.

She came home from school one day to find Mrs. Smith taking Alma's dresses apart. "What are you doing to my dresses?" she asked, with a horrified look on her face.

"These dresses are only fit for the rag bag," Mrs. Smith stated flatly.

"Well, I just wish you had talked to me," Clara said sharply.

"Oh Clara, don't fret so, we'll make you more as time goes on. You've already finished one, and as you have money to buy more yard goods. I'll help you make more. After all, I don't want to be ashamed of you."

Clara was frustrated but was silent after that. She soon left the room and went upstairs to do her homework, but couldn't keep her mind on it. *I loved those dresses Mrs. Conners made,* she thought. *They were so detailed, and the idea of my sweet lady stitching all those tiny stitches by hand. I just wish Mrs. Smith had said something. I would have stopped her.* Later, she was surprised at herself for speaking out the way she did to Mrs. Smith. It wasn't like her, but she had been so hurt at the injustice of it.

As she sat in front of the window at her desk, she opened it and looked up at the stately oak tree outside her window. The leaves were just turning a soft nut brown. They would hang on to the life-giving tree long after the rest of the trees had shaken their leaves off.

I will shake my bad memories off, too, she thought. *I'll hang on to my memories of a better life than I now have and I'll grow up and be the kind of woman Mama would be proud of. I'll remember the values Mama taught me, and I'll teach them to my children. I won't let this time with the Smiths change me. I'll be who Mama, yes, and Father wanted me to be in the beginning.*

She snapped out of her reverie and started her homework. The Smiths would be calling her down for supper preparations and chores soon. She'd better get started.

That Saturday, Mrs. Smith taught Clara to bake pies. As she mixed the dough the recipe Mama used to use came into her mind--2 cups flour, a third of that measure of lard and then a third of that measure of cold water, and add 1 teaspoon of salt. She enjoyed kneading the dough and rolling it out and even remembered the special slits Mama used to make in the middle for venting.

"That's nice, Clara, you made sort of a design. I like that. You really seem like an old hand at pie making. Are you sure you've never made pie before?"

"No, I just watched Mama, that's all." She liked working in the kitchen; it brought back happy memories of her life with Mama and her family, which had been centered around the kitchen.

In time, she was trusted to bake by herself. One Saturday morning Mrs. Smith came into the kitchen as she was making two special pecan pies to surprise them with. They were to have the preacher over for dinner the next day.

"Here, what are you doing wasting all these precious ingredients on these pies?" Mrs. Smith yelled.

"Well, I thought since we were having company tomorrow …"

"Cream pies would have been just fine for the preacher and his family. After all, they're not used to such fine fare."

Once again Clara felt dejected. She thought, *Oh dear, I've done it again.*

Clara lived with the Smiths for more than two years. She continued with the back-breaking labor Mr. Smith imposed upon her, always with a cold sneer on his face which gave her chills, trying to please Mrs. Smith, and going to school and keeping up her studies the whole time. When life got too hard, as it was bound to do at times, she remembered who and whose she was. Her determination gave her a will to stick to it when she felt like giving up and moving back with her family. Always she came to the same conclusion. Her father had enough to contend with. She wouldn't give him more. Her rare visits home convinced her of that. As a result, she never shared her problems with him. Then, in her senior year of high school, a traumatic occurrence happened.

Chapter 21

AS SPRING SETTLED IN the area, Clara's hopes soared. She would be graduating this spring. She did so want to go to college; she wasn't sure just what she wanted to do, but her thirst for learning wasn't satisfied. She loved natural history and science but wasn't sure how she wanted to use them. Her teachers encouraged her to go on to teachers college. "Clara, in only two years you could have a teacher's certificate," they told her.

The Smiths, on the other hand, were oppressive, telling her to look for a beau and settle down. "What's a girl want with all that education anyway?" Mrs. Smith said.

Mr. Smith echoed it with, "Stay here and work on the farm until you find someone to marry you."

Then, two months before graduation, things changed dramatically. A new minister came to the little Evangelical United Brethren church she grew up in. While staying at the Smith farm, none of them attended regularly at the church near them. Clara had been feeling as though God and her parents' training were slipping away. Her father and his family weren't going to church regularly either, since her Father had turned his back on God, and Dora certainly had no inclination for anything to change.

Mrs. Smith was helping Clara with a very sophisticated dress for graduation. She had told Clara she looked better in tailored clothes than frilly ones, so on that basis they picked out yard goods together. They chose tiny gray and burgundy checks with a white background. The dress had pleats on each side in front and back and was trimmed in a solid burgundy at the hips and had a white Peter Pan collar. Clara loved it and was so excited about graduating. She would be receiving an award for excellence and special recognition at the ceremony.

At school that Tuesday Clara was on her way off the grounds when Effie approached her. "Clara, wait a minute. I want to talk to you about something," she said. Clara slowed down and waited for her friend to catch up with her.

"An evangelist is at our church this week, and I would really like you to come and hear him. I heard him at both services on Sunday and then on Monday, and he's really good."

"Oh Effie, how can I do that? The Smiths keep me so busy. Then with my studies and trying to get my dress done for graduation …"

"Come Friday for supper and go with us. Mama would really like to see you again."

That did sound really good. She hadn't Seen Effie's mother in so long. "Okay I'll try. But don't get your hopes up."

The Smiths put up a terrible fuss, but Clara was able to overcome every obstacle.

On Friday she went home with Effie, and it was so good to see kind-hearted Mrs. Dickerson. Clara was sure Mrs. Dickerson was a Christian--she was so like Jesus. Clara also appreciated the good feeling in the home, like God was there.

At services that night, Clara felt Effie was right. There was something special about the evangelist. Although the message was good Clara had a hard time keeping her mind on it. She kept going back to her family, the Conners, and now the Smiths. Maybe she had been wrong to stay with the Smiths. She certainly felt far from God. *I made promises to my mother's memory, but am I keeping them? Mama loved her Lord, and she*

was always so close to Him. I feel bad about where I am now. I haven't even read my Bible in a long time. She resolved to do better.

"None of us are good enough. We all sin and come short of the glory of God," the Preacher boomed. She was dumbstruck. *How could he know?* She thought.

She left the service in a very somber mood. Effie seemed to understand and was quiet, too. That night, Clara hardly slept.

She spent the night at Effie's and was taken home in horse and buggy the next morning.

The Smiths seemed to give her extra work that Saturday, probably to make up for lost time. She went to bed very tired, but restless. Just as she was closing her eyes she heard her door creak. Her heart pounded as she turned over. A large shadow loomed over her. In the moonlight she recognized Mr. Smith. He had no clothes on. He leered at her as he easily stripped the covers from her. She felt frozen in place as he raised her nightgown, and before she could get her thoughts together she felt his hot, sweaty hands sliding up her body. She tried to scream, but no sound would come. He crawled over her and spread her legs. She kicked him between the legs, and as he fell back in pain, she lunged away from him with all that was in her small frame. He grabbed her nightgown, but it only ripped a piece of the cloth as she got away from him. She heard herself whimpering as she flew down the stairs.

Outside she went. She hit the wet, damp grass and headed for the barn. She opened a trap door in the floor and lowered herself down. As she lay there grasping for breath she heard Mr. Smith overhead.

"Clara, I know you're in here. I saw you come in." On and on he talked as she heard him checking every nook and cranny. She could even hear his heavy breathing. "Clara, you might as well come out. I'll find you and make it even harder on you."

It was then that she decided to make a break for it. The barn was built on a slope so the back of the barn had a small door for animals to pass through.

She stole out the door and, like lightening, she ran through an apple orchard and didn't stop for two miles when she reached the neighboring farm. All that heavy work he had her do had paid off.

In the moonlight she saw Mr. Smith running behind her on the edge of the yard. Up the steps and through the front door she went. An old man was bent over in a chair reading the Bible by candlelight.

"Child, what's wrong? You look like you've seen the devil himself."

"Oh I have," she sobbed, falling into the poor man's arms. She somehow got the story out as he fixed her some tea and tried to calm her down. He then got his rifle and went to the porch and scanned the length and berth of the yard but didn't see anything. "The rat's gone back to his hole", he said. "Child, lie down on the sofa and rest. We'll decide what to do in the morning."

"No, I can't. He knows I'm here. Won't you please take me to my friends?" she cried imploringly.

The kind-hearted man wrapped a blanket around her and put socks on her feet. He then brought his buggy around and gently carried her and placed her in it.

Hours later they drove up into the Dickersons' farmyard. The door was opened, and Mr. Dickerson quickly came to life as he saw Clara's face and felt the urgency.

They went into the kitchen and the nightmare was explained to him. Clara was able to relate the story with some coherence by that time.

"Thank you very much for bringing her here, Mr. Van Sweden. Don't worry--we'll take care of her." The dear man became a good friend of Clara's after that night.

Clara was put to bed after she was given a sedative, and she slept until well after dinner the next day. When she woke she bathed and was given some of Effie's clothes and ate a light lunch.

In the kitchen she asked Effie if they were going to church that night.

"Yes, but we won't go now of course."

"But I want to come with you," Clara said.

So they all went to church together that night after she convinced them that she very much wanted to go.

As the evangelist talked about sin and the consequences of it, Clara listened. She thought about how she had come to this point. She heard the preacher say how, little by little, the devil lures us away from God. *Yes,* she thought, *that was true.* How could she live in the Smith home knowing Mr. Smith was evil? Yet still she had let Satan tell her it would work, all the while moving farther from God.

The service ended with an altar call. Sobbing, the preacher pleaded with sinners to repent. "Softly and Tenderly" was sung imploringly.

With a pounding heart, Clara slipped from her seat and went to the altar to ask Jesus to come into her heart, making her a new creation. There and then she dedicated the rest of her life to serving her Lord and she never wavered from her commitment.

As the pastor of the church came to pray with her, she found herself telling this godly man the story of the past few hours.

"You've got to get out of that house tonight. I'll take you myself to get your things," he told her. She didn't want to go, but she knew he was right.

"How can I face them?" she asked.

"I'll be right there with you, and you know, Clara, this has to be dealt with."

Driving through the night, they arrived at the Smith farm. Mr. Smith answered the door. He and Mrs. Smith were just retiring for the night. "Good evening," he said in an irritatingly sweet voice.

"We've come for Clara's things, the pastor said.

"You're not taking any of the dresses I've worked my fingers to the bone over," said Mrs. Smith from behind her husband. This surprised Clara. He must have made up some wild story to give her, she thought. She was taken aback at the unfairness of this since it was she who bought the fabric and made them, but she just wanted to get it over with. She stiffened her back and walked right past Mr. Smith with the pastor right behind her. Her meager belongings, including the precious chest Mrs. Conners had given her, were quickly loaded in the buggy.

The preacher turned to Mr. Smith and said, "If you ever come within shouting distance of Clara again you won't be alive to tell about it!" *Wow,* Clara thought, *strong language for a preacher.*

"Clara," he said on the way home, "men like that have to be talked to plainly. He's evil, and there's no other way to let him know I mean business. Come and stay with our family until you graduate, and then you can decide what to do. I know I speak for my wife. She would love the company, and you could give her a hand now and then."

Thus, it was arranged. Mr. Smith never decided to test the pastor's threat.

Chapter 22

THEY RETURNED VERY LATE to the pastor's home. It was a lovely little stone cottage next to the church. Clara was introduced to his wife, Ruth, who put her arms around Clara and gave her a motherly hug such as she hadn't received in a long while. Clara experienced at once a feeling of warmth and shared intimacy with the caring woman. Pastor Johnson had quickly related the story to his wife before they left for the Smith farm earlier in the evening, but, having themselves been new to the parish, they knew nothing else about Clara. They just accepted her on face value. Ruth seemed to appreciate what Clara had been through and trusted her by instinct.

"I've made up a bed in the guest room. It's quite small, but I hope it will do," Ruth said.

"I'm so grateful to both of you. I hope I can make it up to you," Clara replied.

"There's no need to. We are blessed to help. You've been through so much."

Ruth took Clara to a cheery little room and put her to bed. Clara felt safe and cared for and immediately fell asleep, but not before she thanked her Lord!

When she awakened the sun was shining through a crack behind the blinds at the window. It fell across the foot of the bed as if to gently wake her up. She quickly washed and dressed and went into the kitchen, where Ruth was kneading bread. A cute little towheaded boy with big blue eyes was sitting at the table watching her.

"Well good morning, Clara. Did you sleep well? Ruth asked her.

"Yes I did, but you shouldn't have let me sleep so late."

"You needed it. Clara, this is Billy. He's two, and into everything."

"My, what a beautiful boy he is. Hello Billy," she said, and was rewarded with a smile.

That afternoon Clara met Mary. She looked just like Billy only with the mature look of a first-grader. She was quite shy, the exact opposite of her vivacious younger brother. She had blond pigtails and reminded Clara of herself when she was younger.

Clara, Ruth, and even Mary all worked together to fix supper. Clara had spent the afternoon settling into her room. She didn't feel she could stay here permanently, even though the Johnsons were kind enough to take her in. She felt they were cramped in this small cottage, plus she wanted to earn money this summer for college in the fall.

That evening at church Clara was pleased to see her father and brothers there. She spoke to them before services. Dora's boys had left home to find their way. Clara sincerely wished them well.

It seemed Dora had withdrawn since Hulda ran off to New York with a traveling salesman. *At least Daddy won't be hen-pecked by her anymore, and with her children gone he will get some peace*, Clara thought. She looked at him and saw a yearning, wistful look.

Clara took her seat with Ruth and the Johnson children and prepared to listen to the sermon, hungry for more of God's word.

The evangelist didn't let her down. The scripture was from Job. Job's friends thought because he was good nothing evil could happen to him. So therefore he must have sinned, since things were going poorly in his life. But Elihu put them in their place. "His ways are higher than our ways," Job spoke, without knowing why. Job 42:5-6 says: "My ears had heard of you but now my eyes have seen you therefore I despise myself and repent in dust and ashes."

At the end of the service Clara saw Israel come stumbling to the altar. She rejoiced in her heart, knowing that now he could finally put the death of Inez to rest, knowing she was in the arms of Jesus. Shortly after that, her three brothers all followed their father. Clara's heart swelled to overflowing. It seemed God was drawing her family back to himself, and she was excited by the prospects.

As graduation loomed closer she still had no solution to her future plans. She had to have a place to live, and the thoughts of college still played on her mind. This was something all of her teachers had encouraged her to do, but she had no idea how.

She decided on Sunday after church she would invite herself home to dinner and talk the problem over with her father. That night as she went to bed, her thoughts turned again to college and what she would say to her father.

Pray about it, Clara! Out of nowhere came this thought. It had really been a long time since she had felt intimate with her Heavenly Father, but just then she felt amazingly close to Him. The rest of the week she prayed fervently and asked the Johnsons to do so, also.

So it was that two weeks before graduation from high school, she sat talking to her father after Sunday dinner and dishes. It was a beautiful May afternoon, and they sat on the front porch in rocking chairs. She felt a strong sense of the childhood security she had before her mother died.

"Clara, you know I would love to have you stay here, but I don't know how that would solve the problem of money. I can afford to help you through college, but I can't come up with the whole thing. I remember Uncle Lonz saying Aunt Iva has come down with T. B. and was sent to a sanitarium. Uncle Lloyd is struggling to keep the family together and still hold down his farming. He may be able to pay you to come and help for the summer, anyway."

They agreed that Israel would write to Uncle Lonz and propose that Clara come. The next week, she prayed that she would be able to go up north and help and earn the money she still needed for college. In the meantime, she applied to a Bible school she hoped to afford. This would at least get her started.

By the end of the next week she heard from her father that Uncle Lonz was excited about the prospects of her coming.

So it was arranged that Clara would leave on the train the day after graduation.

Clara was still nervous about going out on her own after the incident with Mr. Smith, but she was determined to go to college, and this did provide a way.

Graduation from high school was a proud day for her. She didn't have the dress that she and Mrs. Smith had worked on, but her best dress was cleaned, starched, and ironed. Clara was busting at the steams with pride in her achievement and the honors presented to her at the ceremonies.

She looked into her father's eyes and saw them glistening with unshed tears. How happy she was to have a restored relationship with her family.

The following Monday morning found her on a train heading to northern Michigan. She renewed her determination to earn money for Bible school in the fall. She again pored over brochures and decided, yes, with careful management, this was a school she could afford.

Chapter 23

As the train sped through Grand Rapids, Clara remembered that day that seemed so long ago now, when she and Aunt Genie had made this same trip. Only now Clara was going on to Tustin A little town up north. It was a beautiful sunny day, and the trip was so enjoyable. The trees were full and lush and the grass a vibrant green. The corn was just up above the ground, covering it like a blanket. She sat and munched on her fried chicken and sipped the lemonade that Dora had graciously packed for her. Then she ate one of the last apples from storage.

With her favorite book in hand, she had a hard time concentrating on it. She laid her head back on the seat and, with a full stomach, let herself be lulled into sleep.

Much later she awoke with the afternoon sun shining in her eyes. She looked out and realized that the lay of the land was much different. The grass was sparse, and it was very hilly and sandy with lots of tall pines. The train was slowing to a gradual stop. *Why, this is my station,* she thought as she read the sign at the little brick building. Quickly, she smoothed her hair and brushed off her dress. As she gathered her things the conductor came through calling for Tustin. "Last call for Tustin," he bellowed.

As she stepped off the train, there was a man with a sign with which read, Uncle Lloyd. A big portly looking gentleman. "Hello, I'm Clara," she said, which was very obvious since she was the only passenger to get off. Clara's belongings were loaded on a nearby wagon by a very relieved-looking Uncle Lloyd.

An hour later they arrived. As they drove up a rather steep driveway, she studied the house. It was mostly built with large rocks, but there were several levels. Some were made with wood, and so were various small buildings scattered around. Everything seemed rather haphazard and crooked.

As they came in through a shed in back to the kitchen they entered the biggest upheaval Clara had ever seen. Dishes were piled in the sink, a dirty dish towel hung carelessly on a chair. The big room was grimy and dull, and this was just the kitchen. "How long has Aunt Inez been gone?" she asked in bewilderment.

"I'm sorry about the mess. She's been gone about three weeks now and wasn't able to do much for quite some time," he said, as he looked around with eyes as a stranger would. Several children were staring at her. "Let me show you to your room. You must be tired."

They bustled around, and Clara was shown to an almost bare room with only necessities in it--bare wood floors, one single bed, dresser, commode, and hooks for her clothes. Dust bunnies were visible under the bed. Nothing had been done in quite some time, but as she turned down the quilt on the bed, the bedding looked clean, so, making the best of it, she settled her things, changed her travel clothes, and went back to the kitchen. One little girl was still there, looking forlorn. "What's your name?" Clara asked kindly, bending down to her size.

"Janice" said the sad little thing, looking at her with big, deep blue eyes as round as marbles.

"Where are the others?" Clara wanted to know.

"They all went out to play," she answered shyly.

"Would you please look them up and tell them I would like to see them in the kitchen?"

One by one they came. Each time she introduced herself and asked their names. One boy, the oldest, and a replica of his Father, said his name was "puddn' tame, ask me again, and I'll tell you the same."

"His name is Wilbur", a thin girl with straw-colored braided hair and freckles said, "and my name is Sandy." A little towheaded boy was William, but they called him Billy.

Clara had noticed several various cats and a dog outside as they rode up. "Who takes care of the animals?" she asked.

"Mama" was the reply.

"Who tends the garden?" She had noticed a very weak, scratchy garden outside the kitchen window when she came in.

"Mama," they said.

"Well, Mama is in the hospital getting better, and when she comes home (faces brightened), we want to have everything in order for her so she won't get sick again, don't we?" She saw nods of approval on each face.

"Then we need a program. Boys, you tend the animals and help your father in the barn. Girls, you'll help me in the house and weed and water the kitchen garden." The kids' eyes boggled with amazement. By this time, Clara was quaking with fear at all she was suggesting. This might not work. She knew her step–brothers and step-sister certainly would have shirked all this responsibility. "Girls, let's put our aprons on." They found clean, but un-ironed, aprons and donned them.

"Boys, go find your dad and see what chores he has for you."

Two hours later the boys came in from the barn.

The kitchen had somewhat been put in order, and a supper of sorts had been put together.

The males ogled it hungrily. Clara looked at the dirty hands and faces. "Right after you wash outside at the well, we'll eat," she said. They humbly filed out of the kitchen, and when they came back, faces and hands were scrubbed clean. They all sat at the table, and after thanks to the Lord for their good fortune, and with great appreciation, ate their meal.

Later that night as Uncle Lloyd and Clara sat in the easy chairs in the kitchen, he talked to her about Aunt Inez. He thought she could probably come home by the end of the summer when Clara would go off to college.

In bed that night, before Clara dropped off to sleep, she thanked God for this job and the fact that the children had responded to her. She really had a desire to help the family. Her thoughts turned to her mother as she closed her eyes in exhaustion. *I will make it, Mama. I will graduate from college! Just stay with me and give me the courage I need. Help me to do this job the best I can.*

Chapter 24

THE NEXT MORNING CLARA was up early, baking four loaves of fresh bread. After breakfast she and the girls set off to find enough gooseberries to bake a pie for supper.

Sandy trudged on ahead eagerly, while Janice matched Clara's stride and shyly took her hand. She looked up into Clara's eyes and smiled, but as their eyes met Clara saw a deep sadness in those pools of blue. Clara remembered how she felt when her own mother died, even the lump in the middle of her stomach and how her throat ached. Clara felt she knew something of how Janice felt, but their mother was coming home again! "Let's make a surprise for Mama when she comes home," Clara suggested. "What shall we make?"

"Well, she loves pudding."

Hiding a smile Clara said, "I'm afraid that won't keep long enough, but how about if we embroider a special kitchen towel for her? We could put her favorite flowers on it with her favorite colors. Janice's enthusiastic nods were all the encouragement Clara needed. They walked on and caught up with Sandy. They found the bushes to be lush with ripe, pungent, and fragrant berries. Janice talked on about the special towel. Sandy joined in on the discussion and she thought she would make her mother a table runner. She would make a tree with Mama's favorite birds.

The morning passed with these plans, and soon they had more than enough berries for the pie and maybe even some jam. They hurried home to fix dinner.

That afternoon Clara put the girls to work straightening up the house and putting things away, carefully instructing them in efficiency, while she started on the mounds of ironing. There was still lots of laundry to be done, but that would have to wait until Monday morning. As Clara worked, she developed a plan to have things running smoothly in the fall when Aunt Inez would hopefully come home and Clara would leave for college. She thought if the children were trained in the basics of running a home, and they all knew their jobs, then when Aunt Inez did come home it would be much easier for her.

Clara was thankful for the training Mrs. Cunningham had given her and, yes, even Mrs. Smith.

Why, thanks to Mrs. Smith she could sew, and there was a sewing machine in the kitchen. Maybe she could use it in the afternoons. She worked on a plan to make new clothes for college. Her father was struggling to help with school so she knew there would be precious little for anything else.

⁂

Mid-morning the next day Janice came in flushed from working in the garden. "Can I have a drink of water?"

Clara knew the pump was right outside and she could have easily gotten one there, but she went to the icebox and took the picture of cool water out for her. "It's getting pretty hot out there, isn't it?" She said as she looked out the kitchen window. "Why don't you sit down a minute and cool off." With a shy smile, Janice did just that.

"I wonder what Mama looks like now," Janice said with a faraway look in her eyes.

Clara was busy making a stew for dinner, so it was a good time for them to talk since she was busy and Janice would have an easier time sharing not having to look Clara in the face.

"Well, I think maybe she'll be more rested and feel much better by now, don't you?"

"Yes I do," the little girl said sounding hopeful. "She'll probably want to make me a new dress for school."

"I'm sure she will, but remember that she hasn't been doing much else but resting. It will take time to build up her strength. We do want her to stay well, don't we?"

"Oh yes. Maybe she won't want to make me a dress for a while. I can wear my old ones to school until then."

"Remember Janice, we are only hoping that she can come home in September. We need to see what her doctor says."

"I'll remember. Can we pray about it tonight, Clara?"

"We will, and we won't stop praying. God will do what he thinks best, though."

"Okay, Clara. I think I will go out and help Sandy now."

Each child separately talked to Clara about their hopes and fears and seemed to be satisfied with her answers.

As summer moved on, things around the house seemed to run smoothly.

Wilbur turned out to be the jokester of the family. He was always pulling some harmless stunt to make people laugh, and Billy seemed to take everything in stride. He missed his mother but seemed able to cope with the assurance that his father was there for him.

Uncle Lloyd was hard-working enough, now that he didn't have to worry about running the household. Clara felt good about herself. The years of hard work seemed to take their toll, but she felt that she was managing quite well. She was still small, not quite five feet tall and underweight, so she benefited from the fresh produce and healthy food she cooked. The meat and dairy that was always available strengthened her. Then there were the vegetables from the garden.

She grew to love the children, and they loved her. Oh, they sorely missed their mother and counted the days until she could return to them, but Clara was a good substitute until their mother would be home again. Years later, Clara still held a warm spot in her heart for them.

In August, Clara received word that she would be accepted into the Bible school in Kentucky and started planning for it. She prayed faithfully that Aunt Inez would be home by then. She wasn't sure what would be done otherwise.

She and the girls were busy canning and drying every available vegetable and fruit. Meat was already canned and salted and put away. In November a hog would be butchered to add to the winter supply.

The men were busy with wood for winter already. Winter usually came early that far north. Soon wheat would be harvested and then corn for animal feed. Farm life was busy indeed.

One morning she and the girls went to pick raspberries for jam. The sun was shining, and the woods smelled of fresh pine after a rain.

Sandra and Janice were exhilarated with the fresh air and abundance of fruit. "Just look," Clara said, "the hill is red with all the ripe fruit!" Janice went a little farther in her excitement over all of the lush, red berries. "You be careful Janice," Clara warned, "stay where I can see you."

"I will," Janice promised. A few minutes later, Clara glanced up and Janice was out of sight. "Where is Janice?" she asked Sandra.

"Well, I don't know. She was right here!"

She just seemed to drop out of sight. The two immediately set off look for her. She was nowhere to be seen. They called and called, but came up with nothing.

The sun was high in the sky. The others would be expecting them home for lunch. Clara's imagination got carried away. She knew bears had been sighted this far north. She didn't think there were poisonous snakes in Michigan. She prayed fervently. Doing so calmed her fears, and she was able to think rationally. "Stay with me, Sandra--don't you get lost, too."

Taking hands, they combed the area. Clara looked worriedly at the sky. More than an hour had passed and still no Janice. She knew that soon she would have to go home and report to Uncle Lloyd. *Oh, he trusted me with his children and now what have I done! I've lost sweet little Janice. She may be in danger.*

Suddenly they came to the edge of a gully, made steeper with the rainfall. At the bottom lay the small tot, motionless. Down they went. Janice was as white as a sheet. She had a cut bleeding on her forehead. Clara quickly tore the hem of her petticoat and soaked it in a puddle of water left from the rain, being careful to stay on top where the water was clean, and dabbed Janice's head with it. Soon Janice came around. "What happened?" she asked.

"You're alright. You just took a tumble," Clara explained.

Clara carried her piggy back home while Sandra carried the berries. Uncle Lloyd was astonished at the tale but pleased they had handled it so well.

All afternoon they worked, putting up the jam and fixing supper and a gooseberry pie for dessert. Janice got to lie on the daybed in the kitchen, resting and enjoying her afternoon off.

To top off the excitement of the day, they received a letter in the mail saying that Aunt Inez was ready to come home, and Uncle Lloyd was to pick her up the following week on Tuesday.

That night, as Clara said her prayers, she thought she must be in the Lord's will for everything to be working out so well.

Chapter 25

IN EARLY SEPTEMBER, CLARA found herself on a train going south. The final goal for her by train was Jackson, Kentucky, where students of the Bible College in the hills of Kentucky would be picked up.

Francis was traveling with her for safety. She had a layover in Cincinnati, which was not considered safe for a lone female traveler. White slavery, which originated in England in the middle of the 19th century, was rearing its ugly head in America during the Roaring 1920's. It was a time of loosening morals on the whole. Young girls were kidnapped, shipped to England, and never heard from again. Once a girl was caught and sold into prostitution, even if she escaped, her life was ruined after being used in such a vile way.

The late summer sun shone through the trees and cast a golden glow on ripened wheat fields. What a golden time of year it was. Clara thought of Michigan and the annual dressing of finery in red, yellow, gold and greens, and wondered if any other place could be so beautiful. *I guess I am about to find out*, she thought.

The two of them had much to catch up on. "Clara, I really feel the Lord calling me into the pastoral ministry," Francis told her. "My heart aches for our country at this time. Satan seems to have been let loose since the fiasco of Abolition and then repeal."

"It really seems like it has just made matters worse, doesn't it? Like when there isn't enough to eat, and then when food is more plentiful you can't seem to get enough," Clara commented.

"It really does seem like it's just made matters worse to try and fight against the drinking of liquor."

"Men's hearts won't be changed without God's intervention, will they?"

"Clara, this is such a burden on my heart. Please pray that if it is God's will, money will be found to accomplish seminary for me."

On they talked, whiling away the hours.

They were planning on staying in a hotel that night. Francis would see Clara off in the morning and continue his journey to a Bible college.

As Clara lay back on her headrest, her mind went to other train rides.

She remembered the time when Mama took her to Grand Rapids to shop for material with her precious egg money.

Then there was the trip she made with Aunt Genie after Mama died. "Francis, do you remember the beautiful green coat Aunt Genie bought me on the trip to Grand Rapids?"

"Clara, I saw Hulda wearing the coat after you left," Francis said. "Her mother certainly didn't do her any favors. Her life is so messed up now, and the boys are regular rogues."

"Francis, why didn't you tell me then?"

"Think about it. Dora would have found some way to outsmart us, and it would have been harder on Father."

"Oh, I'm sure you're right."

As she lay back again, she thought of the trip she had made this summer to care for Uncle Lloyd's family. She thought of what she had taught the children to do, to help run the household. She wondered how they were getting along now. *Yes, they should be able to shoulder enough of the responsibility so their mother can regain her strength,* she thought. *I wonder how little Janice is doing. She seems so vulnerable. I will write to them as soon as I'm settled in school,* she decided.

Both Francis and Clara, tired from the frenzy of packing and leaving, slept the rest of the train ride and woke refreshed. They looked forward to a nice meal at the hotel dining room. What a treat it was to spend time with each other.

When they were settled in the hotel, they went to the dining room and had dinner together and reminisced for far too long into the night. What a satisfying time they had.

The next morning they woke early to breakfast before their separate departures. It was a misty, gray morning. The dingy train station seemed very depressing. As they sat waiting, they noticed a lone traveler who sat on a bench by herself. Clara and Francis both kept glancing her way. How strange she was, alone in such dangerous times. Two men, who looked as if they had slept in their saggy clothes, and had at least a week's growth of whiskers and blurry eyes, appeared out of the darkness and walked in her direction. They kept their eyes trained on the girl.

As Clara and Francis watched, the men seemed fidgety, walking away and then coming back--throwing something in the trash can, smoking cigarettes, pacing, whispering quietly to each other.

"Let's pray," Francis said quickly. "In the name of Jesus," he prayed, "don't let these men even touch her!"

"Yes Father, don't let her life be destroyed. Protect her," Clara prayed.

Then, out of the darkness, keeping their eyes trained on the lone girl, one man reached for her just as a bright circle of light circled her. The man couldn't seem to push his hand through the circle of light.

One man swore, and the other stared in amazement. Someone called for a policeman as the men went running down the street. Later it was learned that they were apprehended.

The station was a bustle of talk after this incident happened. The poor girl sat, visibly shaking. Clara and Francis went to her, as did other others. "Are you alright?" Clara asked her.

"I'm so scared. Mother begged me not to come alone, but I so wanted to go to Bible school. I felt the Lord would protect me."

"Well, he certainly did that. Are you by any chance going to the Bible school up in the hills from Jackson?"

"Why yes I am! How did you know?"

"Well, I'm going there too! We'll go the rest of the way together. What's your name?"

"Mary. It is so nice to meet you both. What a scare, but you know, I felt people praying for me, and I felt so at peace and such a warmth, like God was protecting me."

"Let's sit down a minute and get our bearings. This is my brother Francis. He'll be going in a different way from now on."

Chapter 26

CLARA AND MARY CHATTED all the way to Jackson. They seemed to have a great deal to share with each other. It was almost as if they had been friends for life. Mary came from a small town in Pennsylvania. Her father died when she was very young. He was swept away in a flood when a dam broke above the town. Mary and her mother were saved by a tree branch, which they clung to for days while the water receded. Climbing into the tree, they sat in its branches and even ate the bugs, which were also clinging to the tree for dear life.

"Sounds a little bit like Noah and the ark, doesn't it?" Clara mused.

"Well, after that we really felt like we were saved for something special. I felt like God had something for me to accomplish. That's why I felt it would be safe for me to come on the train alone, that He would somehow protect me."

"Maybe that was part of God's plan, too. It certainly confirms one's faith in God. Maybe he wanted us to meet now."

"Clara, I don't want to be presumptuous, but would you like to share a room with me when we get to the school?"

"I would love to share one with you! It will help so much to already know someone who has a serious relationship with the Lord."

Clara and Mary and several other students were met in Jackson at the train station. Clara was surprised at the primitive horse-drawn farm wagon they were to ride in. Two long benches were built into the sides for seats.

As they looked up into the hills surrounding them, they saw the beautiful fall foliage dotting the hillsides. The trees were stately and brilliant with color. Bird songs could be heard everywhere. They felt overwhelmed with the magnificence of the place. The hills were so steep that the houses hugged the edge of the road and their backyards came to an almost immediate incline. Colorful baskets, abundant with flowers, hung on front porches of the weather-worn exteriors of the houses. Gardens on the sides of them were overgrown with vegetables at this time of year.

Clara and Mary sat on the benches with belongings stacked in front of them. The girls got a kick out of seeing an elderly woman sitting in a rocker on the front porch in a calico dress with a corncob pipe stuck in her mouth.

The ride was so bumpy that before they had gone far every bone in Clara's body ached. On and on they went—one hour, two hours, three hours.

Finally, some of the students, including Clara and Mary, got out and walked, but after awhile that became more difficult as the road grew steep. Then Clara's stomach began to growl. She eventually crawled back into the wagon, as did several other students.

When they started wondering if they would ever arrive, lights from the school came into view.

They were herded out and shown to their rooms, which were primitive and dingy. Clara had packed a patchwork quilt, which helped brighten up the place. She also had brought her precious cedar chest Mrs. Conners had given her, which gave her much comfort. After a fitful night of sleep on an empty stomach, she awoke to rain. As they walked to breakfast in the dining commons, they were drenched. It rained the whole day and then the next. The rain went on for days. The mud was caked to their shoes. At night they felt creepy creatures crawl over them. Beady eyes shone in the dark.

That was the muddiest season Clara could remember living through. Damp, chilled, and depressed, Clara and Mary studied by lamplight before the cold overtook them, and they got in bed to warm up.

Letters from home and Mary's company were the only bright spots for Clara. The mud was almost intolerable. They watched carefully as they walked from building to building so they wouldn't fall in the mud.

By Thanksgiving Clara received a letter from home from her Father.

"Clara, why don't you come home for the holidays? There is a small Bible college in Owosso, Michigan that I think we can manage for the next semester. Then we'll figure what to do from there. Rosemond will be here for Christmas, and you two can get re-acquainted." That's all it took. Clara was eager to leave.

A small group of students were grouped outside the road to go for Christmas vacation. They were to ride the buggy back to Jackson to catch the train. Mary was staying, but had come to say goodbye.

"The one thing I will miss, Mary, is rooming with you. Let's not lose touch with each other."

"No, I don't want to, either. We'll write, of course, and maybe when I'm back in Pennsylvania we can meet someplace in between and have a reunion."

"Oh yes, I would love that. Let's not forget to do it. It would be such fun." The girls hugged, and as the buggy pulled away Mary had tears in her eyes. Clara had a lump in her throat and couldn't talk to anyone for a while.

The train ride was long, and the students stayed together for safety. Each one parted at their respective stops, and in Grand Rapids only one boy was left to protect Clara.

Francis and Walter were there to meet the train. Her belongings were loaded into the buggy, and off they went. The boys were full of news.

Aunt Rilla and Uncle Ernest would be bringing Rosemond home for Christmas. They would be staying a few days for a short visit.

"They are afraid to let her out of their sight. I guess they're worried we'll kidnap our own sister," Walter grumbled.

Which we probably would do," said Francis.

"Well, it would seem she's old enough to make up her own mind now. After all, she is in seventh grade."

"I would love to have her stay awhile. I'm sure in time she would be the same Rosemond we know and love," Clara said.

It was a wonderful Christmas. Father seemed much more cheery now. He was enjoying having all his children home. Dora complained about all the work that was put upon her, but did it. Father was able to not hear the complaining when he didn't want to. Clara supposed after awhile you would just let it roll off your back.

Clara was secretly disappointed in Rosemond. She was selfish and self-willed. What a mess Aunt Rilla and Uncle Ernest had made out of her. She was very beautiful, and she knew it.

Ellen and John came for Christmas, along with their children. Clara remembered how close Ellen was to her mother, who had no sisters, but Ellen, her cousin, seemed like one. The fact that her mother regarded Ellen so highly only added to the warm feeling Clara felt with Ellen there this year.

All too soon it was time for Clara to pack up again and head for Owosso.

Chapter 27

I T WAS AN UNEVENTFUL train ride. She sat back and let her mind go over the most satisfying Christmas she could remember since Mama died. For the first time in years she felt good about her family. Father's situation seemed to work for him. At least she didn't view it as impossible as it was when Dora's kids were living there. Francis was definitely going to a Nazarene Bible College and then seminary. Both Father and Francis felt this was a necessary step, as the Nazarene schools were more affordable than Spring Arbor, a Free Methodist college, and at that it was barely manageable. Francis was disappointed by this arrangement since his grandfather had become Free Methodist and had settled in this area because it was where one of the first Free Methodist churches was established.

Walter seemed content to stay on the farm and help Father, a true farmer at last. Forest was still contemplating what he wanted to do when he graduated from high school.

As Clara daydreamed, she watched out the window at the changing scenery. It was mid-morning in early January, the time of year when harsh winter took a break. The sun shining through the windows seemed especially warm and bright this morning. She watched the stark trees with their dark, moistened bark set against a layer of sun-lit snow. Clara always enjoyed this time of year when the sun seemed to shine more than in November or December. The sky was a brilliant blue, so beautiful it was almost breathtaking.

The train ride proved to be customary, allowing Clara time to catch up on some reading and luxuriate in the warm sunbeams coming through the windows.

At Owosso she took a buggy ride to the school. At the administration building she was given a room key and told she would be rooming with girls named Orpha Case and Nellie Gardener. Her luggage was carried up to the room and left on a bed by the window and a desk. Clara hung her clothes in a small wardrobe, put her folded clothes in the drawers underneath, and settled her chest at the bottom of the bed. All in all she felt very at home. She wondered why the girls had left her the nicest area.

A key rattled in the door and a small, petite blonde with curls spilling from a bun, came through the door. As she smiled at Clara her dimples showed. Clara thought she had the bluest eyes she'd ever seen. They reminded her of the sky she saw on the train ride up.

"Oh, hello, you must be Clara. We've been expecting you. I'm Nellie Gardener."

Clara shook her outstretched hand. "So glad to meet you. I'm Clara Haff."

"Yes, I know, we've been expecting you," she said again and laughed. "How do you like your view? Orpha is practicing selflessness. She wants to be a missionary, so she gave you her spot. She moved her things over there in the corner."

Again the door opened and a tall, stately girl came through the door with the darkest hair and complexion Clara could ever remember seeing. *What a beautiful girl, and so regal!* Clara thought.

"How do you do, I'm Orpha," she said. "I'm so glad you're finally here. We've been expecting you."

The girls sat and talked, getting acquainted. Before Clara knew it, it was time to go to the dining commons.

"Oh dear, we haven't even let you rest," Orpha exclaimed.

"That's all right. I'm sure I'll sleep good tonight, though," Clara commented as she brushed her long auburn hair into buns over her ears. She had developed into a very beautiful woman, just a little short at only 5 feet 2 inches. Her father was especially pleased with the height, since she was so small growing up. She tucked her blouse into a skirt with pleats at the bottom. Her white linen blouse had tiny tucks in front and a frilled stand–up collar with a band. She felt well-dressed and was glad she had taken the time to make some decent clothes last summer. She even made a good dress like the one she and Mrs. Smith had made together. She did not have pleasant memories from that period of time, but time had healed the hurt and she did love that dress.

That semester turned out to be such a good experience. She was so glad her father had arranged it.

She and Orpha became the best of friends. Orpha went on to become a missionary in Africa and never married. Clara and Orpha kept up correspondence most of their lives.

Night after night they stayed up and talked into the wee hours as Nellie slept curled up like a baby. She had a most angelic look on her sleeping face, all pink with her blond hair curled up around it.

A few weeks later Orpha commented, "Clara, I feel the Lord calling me to a deeper walk with him. I want to be totally devoted to him and his will for my life."

"I would like that too. Although I seem so busy. I guess I let things get in my way."

"I know what you mean. I was thinking that after homework each night we could have Bible study and prayer together."

"What a good idea. I would like that!"

And so the girls devoted themselves to that. Clara felt so close to the Lord at that time, like she was really in touch and in tune with God for the first time in her life. She learned the true meaning of servanthood and discipleship. The Bible seemed to come alive for her, and through examples in the New Testament, taught her how to live.

Chapter 28

I N FEBRUARY, AS SHE and Nellie were walking to class together,
Nellie said, "Clara, I'm envious of the relationship you and Orpha
have developed." Never one to be coy or mince words, Nellie came
straight to the point.

"Oh, Nellie, you have such a simple faith. Everything is so easy for
you. You accept everything by faith. You know what you want out of life
and are content to allow the Lord to work in his time. How I envy you
that. Orpha and I struggle with everything. We pray and pray and still
we don't always know God's will in our lives. So we struggle together."

"Well, I guess that's true. I never really thought about it that way."

"You know you want to finish Bible school, get married to some
fortunate man, and bring up a house full of lovely blonde, curly–headed
children."

At that Nellie chuckled. "You sure have me pegged. That's all so
true. Clara, I'm going to pray that the Lord will make clear to you His
will for your life, too."

"Thanks Nellie, I would like that." The girls hugged and had a new
appreciation for each other after that.

That very day Clara's science teacher asked her if she would stay
with his children the following Saturday. He and his wife wanted to
take a trip to Flint and do some shopping. "We should be home by
supper time," he said.

She felt honored that he picked her out of a class of students to do
this. "Yes, I would like to. I'm ready for a change of pace."

On Saturday she got up early and went to breakfast. The cafeteria staff was surprised to see a student so early on Saturday, but got together a decent breakfast for her.

After she arrived at the professor's home, not far off campus, Professor Ewert said, "This is Sally, our inquisitive nine-year-old. This is Benjamin, our very active six-year-old, and this," he said, with a twinkle in his eye, "is baby Anna."

"Oh daddy, I'm not a baby," the girl said with a lisp.

Clara was pleased with the behavior of the children. They were very polite and not rowdy.

"We should be home by dark, but don't worry if we're not," said Mrs. Ewert.

"There's vegetable soup in the ice box and fresh bread in the bread box in the pantry. Oh, and cookies in the cookie jar if they eat their lunch well."

"Don't worry, we'll be fine," Clara said as they went through the door.

"Well, what shall we do first?" Clara wanted to know after the parents left.

"Let's work on our scrapbooks," said Sally.

"That's what she always wants to do," Anna, with big deep blue eyes, informed Clara.

"Well, that sounds like a good place to start."

The children got out their scrapbooks and laid them on the kitchen table. They revealed the children's hobbies. Sally's had bugs, pressed flowers, and leaves.

Benjamin's had things like baseball pictures from newspapers and even an autograph of one sports star.

Anna liked to draw. Hers were mostly her own drawings of her family, her house, and animals.

They inserted more of the things in scrapbooks, while getting acquainted with each other, and then had lunch. In the afternoon they went sledding on a nearby hill.

Clara enjoyed herself immensely. The family even had a wise cat named Samantha. "Sam for short," Anna informed her.

All too soon the day ended, and Clara was driven back to the dormitory.

⁂

Many times after that Clara was asked to stay with the children. When the weather turned mild, they were able to get out for nature walks and the like.

It was a lovely arrangement. Clara was pleased to be earning so much money, and the Ewerts were happy to be able to go out more.

One day in the spring Clara and the children went walking through the woods, finding all sorts of life, both plant and animal. She felt so content and happy being in the woods and with the children. From nowhere she heard a voice say, "you were a born teacher."

Yes I am, she thought.

⁂

Clara searched the library to learn of a teacher's college within a reasonable distance and became convinced and then excited about one in Kalamazoo--Western State Normal school.

She wrote to her father about her plans.

Anxiously checking the mail for two weeks, she finally heard from him. "Clara, I am very pleased with your decision, and I know your mother would be, too. We will work on a plan and maybe if you can work this summer it will be possible."

As the semester wore on, things became pretty routine. Spring was finally in the air. The birds came back and started singing their mating calls. Robins hopped around looking fat and very pleased with themselves, picking up nesting materials and flying off with them. Mosses once again grew in the woods. Trees attained a light green fuzzy appearance.

As Clara and Nellie walked together to class one day, Clara noticed how pale Nellie's face was becoming, the once-pink cheeks were gone and there was no longer a sparkle in her eyes.

"Nellie, are you feeling alright?" Clara didn't want her to make her feel worse, but she was concerned.

"Oh, yes. I've been feeling tired lately, but I think it's just the hard winter and all the hours of study." Clara didn't say any more but she kept an eye on her friend.

Later that day Clara had a chance to talk to Orpha. She listed all the things that concerned her about Nellie.

"I've noticed that, too. She seems to sleep so much, and have you seen how loose her skirts are becoming?"

"Maybe we should talk to Professor Hamilton about it. She respects him, and he can talk to her about seeing a doctor."

The pprofessor did talk to Nellie about it but was unable to convince her to seek medical help.

"I think maybe she is probably afraid of them finding anything wrong," Orpha said.

A few weeks later the three of them were having lunch in the cafeteria. As Nellie carried her tray to the table, to their horror, she fainted, spilling her tray of food.

A student ran to get help. Together with a teacher, she was helped to a chair.

"Nellie, whether you like it or not I have to call your parents," the teacher said.

Reluctantly, she allowed her father to come and get her for a good medical examination. The following week the girls received a letter from her father informing them that the conclusion of the test revealed that Nellie had leukemia and would not be returning to school. There was a letter enclosed from Nellie, expressing her sorrow at not being able to return at the time. She very much hoped to do so in the future. She requested them to pray that she would be able to. She wrote, "I will never forget the wonderful friendship that you two extended to me.

What a privilege it is to have been able to share a room with you. I pray that you both will attain your dreams. I love you, Nellie."

It was just before the end of the term that the girls learned that Nellie had passed away.

Clara had a hard time with this news. How could God allow such a beautiful life to be snuffed out in her prime, before life really started? It was so devastating to Clara. So many people she loved had been taken away.

One night, as she was praying, God reminded Clara of all of the blessings he had given her. She had known her mother for eleven wonderful years, the best part of her childhood. She had brothers and a sister and a father who loved her. She had a place to stay while growing up, a way to get her education, and all this was just the beginning! "Clara, you will see your mother and Nellie again and your little sisters and all the people you love," a voice seemed to say.

"Well, I guess I need to trust God in this," she later told Orpha. "Someday I will know fully, but I sure don't understand now."

Before the end of the year, Professor Ewert came to her. "Clara, I know you are planning to go to a teacher's college in the fall, but how about staying with us this summer? Trudy can use your help, and we would like to take some short trips by ourselves. We know the children would be in good hands with you. We would be able to give you a regular salary, and I presume you can use the extra money for school next year."

To Clara this seemed like the answer to her prayers, and she immediately wrote to her father. He was all for the plan but disappointed that they wouldn't be seeing her more often over the summer.

Clara and Orpha had a hard time saying goodbye. As Orpha left for the summer, they knew they wouldn't see each other in the fall. Orpha would be leaving for missions training. It had been such a close relationship. They seemed to share everything, and their hearts seemed to connect, but finally, it was time to part. After a tearful departure they waved goodbye, promising to write often.

Chapter 29

ONCE AGAIN CLARA FOUND herself on a train, this time on the way for her final leg in her education to become a teacher. *Mama would be so proud of me. How I miss her. Maybe she can see me,* she thought. *Are you up there watching me, Mama? There are so many things I would like to talk to you about.* Sighing, she sat back and remembered other times on the train. The treasured trips with her mother to Grand Rapids to purchase the much-needed supplies not found locally, the well-remembered shopping trip with Aunt Genie, her trip up north to rescue Uncle Lloyd from the hectic life of keeping house as well as the farm, her time at Owosso Bible College, and her dear friends there.

It was hard to leave the Ewerts. They were so considerate and generous to her, and it was especially hard leaving the children. She had become so close to each of these dear unique little ones. They were the ones who made her realize she wanted to teach children, something she had long ago decided but had lost along the way. She wondered how they were getting along now. It really hadn't been that long since she left them, but it seemed so long, and she missed those precious little ones.

Then the last train ride to visit her family was a special time. Rosemond had been allowed to stay for the summer. Of course Dora tried to enlist her help in the work, but it proved to be more trouble than it was worth all in all, and Clara had an enjoyable visit. Now, after a tearful send-off, Clara started looking forward to a new chapter in her life. Living in a boarding house would be a new experience for her, and she had learned of a trolley to the center of town. What fun it all sounded, and sort of an adventure.

"Next stop Kalamazoo," the conductor called, startling her out of her daydreaming. She was picked up from the train station in an automobile, of all things. The trip through town was both helpful and fun. She loved her farming country, but cities were always intriguing to her.

Mrs. Doolittle, the boardinghouse owner, showed Clara around, and then left her on her own. Clara looked around a very up-to-date, ornate, and spacious house facing Vine Street. It was three stories, her room being on the second floor. The walls were covered with old rosebud wallpaper and ruffled organdy curtains at the windows. The furniture was a pretty dark cherry wood, and down the hall there was indoor plumbing. It was the first Clara had ever seen.

Dinner was at 6:00, she had been told, so she unpacked and made herself comfortable in a chair at a small desk at the window. The view was pleasant, looking down at the gardens in back. She saw a bench along a path she would surely make use of. Feeling very dirty and tired from the train ride, she took a bath and then a nice nap, feeling more like herself afterward.

At 6:00 she went to the dining room, curious to meet the other boarders. It was a large room, containing a big table with ten other people seated around it. The meal was simple fare and very good. Clara realized how hungry she had become. Everyone was very congenial, and there was a lot of small talk. The two young girls were Laura and Catherine, Western students who were becoming teachers also. This was their second year here. A man from France, named Morris, also attended the college and wished to settle in this country. He was very intriguing and gave her a looking-over. Clara tried not to notice. He seemed a little older. She was introduced to a Mr. Clark, a businessman who worked downtown, and there was a spinster lady, Miss Edwards. She was very plain and drably dressed. There was Mr. Gates, a salesman who traveled and used the boardinghouse as his home base. He was a middle-aged man with dark elusive eyes and dark hair, bald on top. He wore suspenders over a white shirt, opened at the collar, and black elastic bands on his elbows to hold his sleeves in place. There was a young married couple, Dave and Mary Stouts. They were much more involved with each other than with the rest of the boarders. Clara guessed they hadn't been married very long. There was a single teacher named Miss Adams. Finally, there was a lady with white hair wound around on the crown of her head. She had blue, faded, but sparkling eyes. Her face was lined with deep laugh lines. She was introduced as Mrs. Wellington. Clara thought she was going to like Mrs. Wellington.

After pudding for dessert they sat around and talked until finally Clara excused herself and went to her room. She sat at her desk and wrote a letter to her father, telling him about the boarding house and her safe arrival. She readied herself for bed, knowing she had a big day tomorrow. Between classes she would be checking in with the manager of the cafeteria where she was promised a job working in the kitchen on lunch hours.

Kneeling beside her bed she prayed, and then she had a conversation with her mother. *Mama, there's so much to tell you. Can you see me? Here I am in a nice, comfortable boardinghouse on the final lap of my education. I feel like I can make it, Mama! Can you see me? I will get my teaching degree and become a teacher. I hope you're proud of me.* Then, throwing the window open to look at the stars, she felt as if her mother somehow knew. A peaceful feeling came over her. She crawled into bed and fell into a deep sleep.

Chapter 30

EARLY THE NEXT MORNING Clara got up and got ready for a new exciting day. She washed and dressed and tided her room. She looked around and thought, *My, how fortunate I am. How did I get to this place? God is so good. He's up there watching out for me. How can I fail at anything as long as I stay in His will? She stood* with her hand on the doorknob and looked around one last time. What a nice room!

At breakfast, everything was substantial and filling. Everyone was congenial, although not all of them were here this morning.

It was a lovely walk to school; she took a lift up to the building, which stood high on a hill. Her first class was English literature, which she thought she was going to enjoy. The professor seemed interesting and lively. After that she hurried to the cafeteria to check in with the manager. "Oh, I'm sorry Clara, all of the positions have been filled," the manager said as soon as Clara introduced herself.

"But I understood from your letter that you would hold a position open for me during the lunch hour," Clara protested.

"I couldn't keep it open indefinitely now, could I?" the manager said emphatically as she walked away.

The rest of the day Clara pondered what to do. *Well, I can't stay at the boardinghouse, that's for sure. My money just won't last. I'll tell Mrs. Doolittle tonight and then make some plans.*

She walked home and found her landlady in the kitchen making pies. "How did your first day go, Clara?"

"Oh, Mrs. Doolittle I'm afraid I have bad news. You see, the job I was promised in the cafeteria didn't work out. The manager didn't keep the job open for me as she promised."

Mrs. Doolittle stopped rolling pie dough and looked at her in surprise.

"So you see, I won't be able to afford to stay here."

"But what will you do? where will you go?"

"Well, I haven't worked that out yet, but I've paid you for the week, so that gives me a little time."

"Can you cook?"

"Yes."

"Here, let's see what you can do with this pie crust." Startled, Clara took the rolling pin and finished rolling it out. Mrs. Doolittle then gave her a pie pan, Clara put the dough in, and Mrs. Doolittle poured the blackberry filling in. Clara rolled out the top, venting the crust, as Mrs. Doolittle dotted the topping with butter and slid it to Clara. Clara put the top crust on and finished the pie.

"Anyone who can make a pie can cook! You've got the job."

"What job?"

"Here, of course, with me. You can come home from school and help serve supper, help with dishes after, and with the cleaning on Saturday morning, and we'll be even. I can even give you a little pin money," she said as an afterthought.

"Are you sure?"

"Of course! This is a big job, running the boardinghouse by myself. You can even pack your lunch for school," she said as she pulled out the oven rack for the pies. "Your rent will be a small amount. Less than you can find anywhere else. Well, would you like the job?"

"I would love it, and I can't thank you enough."

"Just do a good job."

As they served the meal the guests seemed genuinely pleased with the arrangement.

Over the next few days Clara noticed Morris watching her every move as she served the meal and felt a fluttering of her heart every time. Then when she sat down at the table, she felt his eyes on her. Dark flashing eyes that smiled. Clara smiled back, but it was very unnerving for her. She didn't know why. She had had male friendships, but she hadn't felt like this before.

"I think Morris is sweet on you," Mrs. Doolittle said one night as they washed dishes together.

"I'm sure he's just being friendly," Clara said. "He's older, and I'm sure he has had lots of chances with other women".

"Well, it looks like he wants a chance with you."

Clara blushed and stopped talking about it.

That night, however, doing her homework, Clara couldn't keep her mind on what she was doing.

It was a Saturday afternoon, and Clara sat at her desk doing homework. She watched out her window as the small animals scurried about up and down trees, tumbling after one another on the ground. She decided to take her assignment out on a nearby bench to enjoy the afternoon with them. It was such a serene garden. Mrs. Doolittle had a special pride in it and it showed. *This is where she gains her sense of peace*, Clara thought. *Everything is laid-out with such thought and care, and I feel it. What a beautiful place to study*, Clara thought as she walked out and sat on the bench she had seen from her window. She found it a wonderful place to study and after that went there often.

One afternoon it was especially lovely. Clara had a hard time concentrating as she watched the birds flittering about and singing. They seemed to be thrilled with the last of summer's warm days. She became entranced as she watched two little ground squirrels play.

"Hello Clara! Enjoying a bit of fresh air?" She looked up to see Morris smiling down at her.

I'm afraid I'm having a hard time studying," she said as he sat down beside her. Again Clara felt her heart fluttering.

"So, how are you finding your classes?" he asked with his wonderful French accent.

What a nice sound his voice made as he rolled the words out, she thought. They told each other about their classes. She asked him about a particular class that she was interested in taking later. As he answered her she looked up at him, listening to his answer. "What lovely sparkling eyes you have," he commented. She blushed and looked away.

They sat talking and enjoying the afternoon together.

Finally she said, "Well, I'd better go back to my room and get serious about this homework," and she stood up.

"Clara I'm going to the park tomorrow afternoon to listen to a concert. Would you like to come along?"

"Yes, I'd love it! I haven't been to the park yet."

"Yes, I noticed you kept your nose to the grindstone, as you Americans like to say."

Up in her room she still couldn't concentrate. She glanced at the clothes on the pegs on the wall. *What shall I wear?* She wondered. *I do hope this weather holds.*

She looked in her mirror and critical eyes looked back at her. *I do wish I were a little taller. He's so tall. All right, let's get serious about your assignments or you won't be going to the concert at all,* she told herself.

Chapter 31

CLARA SAT ON A bench enjoying the concert in the park. It had been a lovely walk over. Having rained the night before, everything was rinsed off and seemed so fresh. The sweet nutty fragrance of the trees and fallen leaves, the moist soil and grass, still green, was sweet-smelling.

She had a sense of wellbeing sitting there. She had chosen her high school graduation dress, which was still looking lovely as she reserved it for special occasions. She considered this concert special, so she gave herself permission to wear it. This was her first date. She had kept her nose to the grindstone, as Morris said. Her studies and just surviving had been major for her. Now here she was on the final lap. *My, if Mama could see me now. Maybe she does. On my final phase in education, sitting here in the park with a handsome man.* She let her senses sway with the music, feeling very good about life.

As Clara and Morris walked back to the boardinghouse, Morris impulsively bought her an ice cream cone at a vendor on the street corner. What a grand day it was.

In the weeks to come they saw each other as often as they could. One beautiful fall Saturday afternoon Clara and Morris went to Milham Park, a large rambling park south of town. The trees were at the peak of brilliance in color. The air was fresh and slightly cool. They walked around and fed the animals peanuts. The bears were glistening with their new coats, ready to hibernate in winter. Clara and Morris walked down the hill on steps holding hands. *How comfortable,* thought Clara, *and right this feels with my hand in his.*

After awhile they sat on a bench and watched the swiftly flowing water sparkling and singing happily. Clara told him about her childhood on the farm and Thornapple Creek running along their propriety and what adventures they had. He smiled and enjoyed the stories and asked questions.

"What was your childhood like?" she wanted to know.

"Oh, not as fun as all that," he answered.

"Did you go to church?"

"Yes, sometimes we did." She never seemed able to get him to talk about his childhood.

"God is very important to me, Morris. I want to serve him always."

"Well, when you look around you see God. He's all around us. But, let's keep walking. We still have much of the park to cover."

Before they returned to the boardinghouse she asked him to attend the little church she had found with her in the morning.

"I will be very busy in the morning, Clara. That's my best study time." A feeling of hurt and foreboding came into Clara, but she said nothing.

Still they saw each other over the next few months and deepened their relationship. Morris did attend services at the little church after a time, but he seemed so uninvolved in the act of worship.

Clara invited Morris home for Thanksgiving and enjoyed the trip. She was happy to show him off to her family.

Father and her brothers seemed quite pleased. Father showed Morris around the farm, and he seemed quite interested.

Thanksgiving was a huge success. Dora was reasonably cordial and everyone seemed to have a good time.

"So, Francis, what are your plans after you graduate?" Morris wanted to know.

"Oh, I'll go to Bible school, then seminary."

"It's all set then, Francis?" Clara asked.

"Yes, Father and visited a Nazarene seminary, and we think it's manageable."

"Oh, I'm so glad, Francis. I know you're making the right decision. You're cut out for the ministry."

"Well, as you know, I've felt God's call on my life for a long time."

"Rosemond may be home for Christmas," Father said.

"Well good! They are so hesitant to let her come, like we would kidnap her. She's ours for Pete's sake," Forest grumbled.

"Well now, let's be reasonable. They did take her at a time when I wasn't able to care for her," Father said.

"Well then they spoiled her so badly she would never want to come home."

"Forest, let's not discuss it now in front of our guest," Father stated with finality.

"Morris, would you be interested in milking a cow in the morning?" Father wanted to know.

"Why yes, I believe I would, but I have never even been to a farm, let alone milked a cow."

"We'll show you," Walter said with resolve.

Saturday afternoon they all went sledding until it grew cold and started to get dark.

Clara almost had the feeling she was back in time when Mama was alive. But no, that would never be.

Things got back into a routine at school. Clara enjoyed her studies and financially, things were working out.

Morris and Clara went to a play at school and enjoyed the Christmas season. They did visit the farm again at Christmas.

Christmas morning they all exchanged gifts.

Clara made Morris a warm muffler to keep his neck warm. She anxiously opened hers from him.

"Oh Morris, this is too much," she said as she opened his gift to her. She took off the lid and there was a beautiful shining white gold watch, intricately carved. She had never owned a watch in her life.

"Clara, I want you to have it as a token of my affection for you. Please accept it."

She happily put it on and everyone admired it greatly.

Chapter 32

T HE NEXT TERM WAS a busy one. Clara was a very conscientious student and enjoyed her studies, especially natural science. She worked diligently for Mrs. Doolittle, who was very pleased with Clara and became a mother figure to her. She and Morris continued to see each other when they could, often walking, talking, going to concerts, and generally enjoying each other's company as often as they could.

Spring came slowly to Kalamazoo. Such a tease it was. One day it would seem a little spring-like and the next would be snowing and blowing and cold. Finally the warmer temperatures won out and signs of spring were evident. Trees turned a fuzzy green, robins hopped around digging for worms to fatten their bellies for their coming families. Spring flowers showed their knobby heads and lovely faces. People became happier without realizing it. Spring was blooming in Michigan.

One day Clara received a letter from Orpha. She was going on the mission field to Africa. How exciting! The two friends hadn't seen each other often and letters were sporadic at best, but they would always hold a special place in their hearts for each other. Clara put the letter in her pocket to be savored later while alone in her room.

That evening Clara opened the letter, sitting in her overstuffed chair, and read it again. How Clara had missed her soul mate. She looked forward to some late night talks. "I am coming to Kalamazoo after school is out for the year", Orpha wrote. "I want to have a good visit and meet your young man." Clara gulped and felt a moment of apprehension. *What will she think of Morris? I know that they will like will like each other*, she thought, but still she had this nagging feeling which she couldn't seem to shake. But her excitement grew as the time drew near.

Clara and Morris both busied themselves with end-term exams. Morris was graduating this year in economics. He was to graduate with honors.

One Saturday evening in June, Morris and Clara took a long walk. "Clara, I've been wanting to talk to you for a while. Let's sit here on this bench and watch the stars come out. It's such a beautiful balmy night."

"Oh my, yes, the trees are such a pretty bright green this time of year, and oh look at the garden over there; the flowers have started blooming. I do love this time of year."

"Clara, if you are quiet a moment I will tell you that I love you. You have won my heart. I'm not sure where I'll be after I graduate. I've applied in Boston, Chicago and Cincinnati, and I'll take the most promising offer. But I want to marry you and take you with me."

"Oh Morris, I love you too, but I still have a year to finish school, and I do want to finish it here. The program is so good, and I know Mrs. Doolittle is counting on me."

"Oh hang Mrs. Doolittle! She'll survive."

"She was so good to me when I needed her. I can't just leave her. She's counting on me, and, as I said, my schedule is all set for next year."

"Well I suppose I could leave and take the job. You could join me in a year."

Clara felt badly. She knew how much she would miss Morris, and she felt a little hurt that he had given in so easily. They walked back and told Mrs. Doolittle and the boarders that they were going to be married. Of course, they were all pleased.

"Mrs. Doolittle, I will be here next year of course," Clara said.

"I'll be taking a job out of town, hopefully in Boston," Morris added.

"How wonderful, but we will miss you," said one of the girls.

"But we don't want to hold you back", the middle-aged salesman stated.

So, the excitement and the plans went forth. Clara was happy, but still that little nagging feeling kept surfacing.

That night before bed Clara said her prayers and read her Bible. She noticed the bright stars out the window and looked heavenward.

Mama, can you see me? she thought. *I'm being married to a wonderful man, and this time next year I will be a teacher. Remember all my schoolteachers, how much they all encouraged me? I want to be like them, and like you Mama. I've loved you so much. You were such an influence on my life.*

Clara went to sleep with a whole range of emotions. Oh, but she did love Morris. He was so handsome and so good to her.

The school year ended, and they both had passed their classes with high marks.

Morris was at the top of his class and received an offer from the firm in Boston, plus the other two. He accepted the one in Boston and would be leaving the first of August. Clara would then go to the farm until fall term started.

Orpha was due in Kalamazoo on July 15. For Clara, the excitement mounted as the young couple spent the relaxed days after graduation together. Everyone around her thought they already knew Orpha because Clara had talked so much about her.

Finally, the big day arrived. Morris went along to the train station to pick up Orpha.

She primly stepped off the train, and Clara was beside herself with joy. "Orpha, over here," she said, and then went running as Orpha ran to meet her. The two soul sisters hugged and wept.

Morris took them to a fine restaurant to eat. The food was excellent, a wonderful French dinner. "Morris this is so good," said Clara

"Of course, Clara, I told you French cooking was the best." The three laughed and talked and had a great time.

That night the girls sat up in Clara's room and talked late into the night. "Tell me everything, Orpha! When do you leave for Africa?"

"My ship sails from New York on July 24. It will take four weeks to get there and then I'll have a train ride across country to Nairobi. I'll be teaching children in a school there."

"Oh, it all sounds so exciting. God sure had you marked from the beginning, but I'll miss my friend so far away."

"Clara, we must never lose track of each other, I promise I will keep in touch whatever I'm doing. I will write and tell you all about it. I'll send a picture of myself dressed in African grab with the children."

They laughed and hugged. "How long can you stay?" Clara asked.

"Only a few days. I'm sorry, but I did want to see you and your boardinghouse and meet your young man."

"Now that you've met him, tell me truthfully. What do you think of him?"

"Clara, I think he's a wonderful man. I can see why you love him, and I think he loves you." Here was the foreboding Clara felt earlier.

"Orpha, I want to know what you are thinking."

"Oh Clara, I want you to be sure his walk with the Lord is the same as yours."

There it was. This is what had been lying under the surface all along. Clara had felt this herself. Orpha had been here less than a day, and she put her finger on it.

"Orpha, I can't get him to talk about it. He just keeps skirting around it."

"Clara, I can see how much you love him, but I have seen marriages that are unequally yoked. I've seen a lot of hurt and suffering, even with my own parents. My mother was ridiculed and belittled by my father all my life. I'm sure at one point they both were like you and Morris, young and in love, but after the newness and thrill of marriage wears off, it's work and commitment, and you both will need common goals. Oh Clara, all I'm asking is that you think about it and pray about it."

"I will, Orpha, and I know it wasn't easy for you to talk to me about it and you thought and prayed about it before you did. You are my dearest friend."

Chapter 33

I N BED THAT NIGHT Clara couldn't sleep. She tried counting sheep, breathing deeply, but nothing would help. Her mind kept returning to her relationship with Morris. What was it based upon? Would it sustain them for a lifetime? Would they have that long together? Over and over her mind went. She looked over at Orpha in the moonlight and saw her sleeping peacefully. Crawling out of bed, Clara sat at her desk and looked up at the starlit sky. *Mama, it's me again. Can you see me? do you know what I'm feeling in my heart? I love Morris so much, but I don't want to be disobedient. I love God, and I want to serve him always. I've grown so close to him. Well maybe there is a little distance since Morris and I ... where did that come from? ... is it true?* She knelt and tried to pray. Growing cold, she realized that she'd been on her knees for almost an hour. Finally she was able to submit her relationship with Morris to God. She would talk to Morris and learn exactly where he was coming from, and if he wanted the same relationship with God as she did. A ring of three is so much stronger than what they would have without a mutual love for Jesus Christ. She knew that.

The next few days were busy. Clara showed Orpha around town, and they caught up on all that had happened since the girls parted last time. Before they knew it, it was time to take Orpha to the train station.

They wept and tearfully said goodbye, not knowing when they would see each other again. Clara watched as the train pulled away.

She could still see Orpha waving her handkerchief out the window, and then she was gone.

The ride home was very quiet. Clara's heart was heavy. "Clara, I think we need to get together tonight and talk seriously. The time is slipping away so quickly," said Morris.

"Yes, I think so too. We only have a few days left."

After supper they held hands and walked to the park.

"Such a peaceful time of day," Clara remarked.

"Let's sit here on this bench and talk. I'm leaving for Boston on Friday."

"Oh, leaving so soon."

'Yes, the time has flown, I know. I'll get an apartment and set up housekeeping. I can probably come back for Christmas, We'll spend it at the farm, and of course we'll write."

"Oh, I'll write every day, Morris. However, there is something I would like to talk to you about before you leave." He looked at her with puzzlement on his face. "Since I was a young girl I have been devoted to God. I went to the altar as a teenager in church and asked forgiveness for my sins and promised to serve Him always. He is first in my life, and I want to know it's the same with you. Otherwise I think our marriage would eventually separate us emotionally."

"Oh Clara, I believe there is a God up there somewhere. I don't believe he has a relationship with us, or we with him. He watches his world and mankind, but not us individually. We can still have a wonderful marriage, though. I don't see how that would cause any separation between us."

"Morris, maybe you will come to change your mind in the future. I don't want you to close it out. Pray about it. Morris, you could come to change your mind and invite Him into your heart," Clara said hopefully.

"But Clara, I haven't sinned and don't intend to tell him I have. I would love to accommodate you, but make no mistake, I won't change my mind, but we can still have a very good marriage."

"Morris it hurts so much to say this, but I can't marry you unless you change your mind and reconsider."

"Clara, don't try and get me to change my mind that way. This is how I was brought up and this is how I will remain!"

She was so hurt to think he thought she was playing games with him. "I'm sorry, but I can't marry you under these conditions," she said with a heavy heart. Orpha was right.

He got up and started walking back, and she followed. The walk home was very strained. They hardly said a word to each other.

He left the following Friday, and she was left with a broken heart.

She traveled to the farm for the few days before school started, feeling so very lonely, like a part of her had been ripped off. She hated going home and telling everyone they had parted ways.

Francis was still there but was getting ready to leave. One morning they walked down to Thornapple Creek, and she was able to tell him all that happened between Morris and her. "I love him so much, and I know life would be good with him, but I know I must put Christ first in my life."

"Clara as hard as it is now, I know someday you'll look back and know you did the right thing. God will reward you for your faithfulness, and it will get easier," Francis encouraged her.

"Oh, Francis I hope you're right. Right now I feel so hurt. I don't understand Morris' attitude."

"I think there are some people who are so proud and independent that they harden their hearts and refuse to give God reign in their lives. The first chapter of Romans tells of this. I think Morris may be one of them. I've sensed this all along with him."

"You are probably right. I fear it's true with him, but it's so hard. My heart is breaking."

He embraced her and let her cry.

Two weeks at the farm steeled Clara for her return to Kalamazoo. With a broken heart, she went through her days. She visited the farm animals. They had always given her so much joy.

In the barn was a new batch of kittens. One fluffy white one with blue eyes came to her to be picked up. She sat on a bale of hay holding the warm, purring creature close to her and rubbing its soft fur against her face. The tiny kitten seemed to know she needed comfort and it nestled up to her.

By the end of the week it rained. She looked out the kitchen window and felt as bleak inside as the weather looked outside. At night she looked into the sky and felt deserted. No stars or answering deity or soft voice of her mother.

Father tried to talk to her, but she couldn't respond the way she knew he wanted her to.

Finally she returned to school and her room in the boardinghouse. People were both curious and sympathetic. They tried to comfort her, but everything seemed so dreary to her.

Fall, usually her favorite season, crept in, but she couldn't seem to snap out of her gloom.

November looked bleaker than ever. She spent the holidays with her family, but her heart wasn't in it. On Christmas everyone was there, even Rosemond, who was now living in Battle Creek. Of course Clara was glad to see her, but still the depression remained.

"Rosemond, I'll be practice teaching in Richland not far from you. Maybe we can see each other then," Clara told her sister. The prospect of this seemed to cheer both girls up.

⚜

Back at the boardinghouse in early January Clara said farewell to yet another temporary home.

Mrs. Doolittle cried openly to be losing her. "Clara, you've been like a daughter to me. Please come back and see me." The boarders were all sad to see her go, too.

"I'll miss your pies," said one.

"I'll be back the week of graduation, of course," Clara reminded them.

"We will all be looking forward to seeing you." *And in better spirits, I hope,* thought Mrs. Doolittle.

Chapter 34

THE FAMILY CLARA STAYED with in Richland was a young farm family, the Scotts. They lived just a mile from town, across the road from his parents, on land given to them as a wedding present from his parents. They were a cheerful couple with two grade school girls and a baby boy.

Richland, as the name implied, was a land of promise and a strong and successful community. It still possessed a one-room schoolhouse, however, and an aging teacher, Miss Crumb.

Because it was too cold to walk to school that January, Clara and the two little girls were taken each morning in horse and buggy, still the most reliable form of transportation. The word was that it was one of the coldest months on record.

The girls were chubby and angelic-looking, with dark brown curly hair combed into pipe curls every morning, and big brown eyes. They always wore frilly dresses ironed to perfection. Martha was slightly taller than Mary and one year younger.

There were twenty-five grade school children, including several mischievous older boys in the back of the room. Miss Crumb was having a hard time handling them.

Clara's bedroom was on the north side of the house. Any sunshine therefore evaded it. She thought this was just fine. It matched her lost, lonely feeling.

One evening she sat at her window, looking across the snowy fields where several large blackbirds were searching for any kernels of corn left there.

Oh, Lord I'm so lonely and lost, she prayed. *I miss the boardinghouse and Mrs. Doolittle and especially Morris. I know that I did what I had to do, but I wish there were another way. I love him so. Everyone has someone; I feel so alone.* She lay down on her bed and wept. Suddenly she heard a voice. *You have me. I will never leave you or forsake you. Trust in me.* She felt a peace like she hadn't experienced in a long while. There was hope.

Yes, I will absorb myself in your work and in prayer. You will help me. You will be my helpmeet.

She watched as the birds flew away together. God would lift her and bring people into her life and give her a man who loved his God and loved her. She felt strength from that resolve.

In school the next day she saw each child as unique. It was like a light came on. She looked at Elma near the back of class. She had a thin and pale unkempt look about her. Her large dark blue eyes were too big for her thin face. The children were eating lunch, and Elma's was nothing but scraps put together.

"Oh dear, I'm much too full for these cookies," Clara said. "Who would like them?" Several hands went up, including Elma's uncertain one. Clara stood up and took them to her.

"That's not fair," said one of the bigger boys in back. "You didn't give us a chance." Clara looked at his large lunch and said, "I guess I can give my cookies to whomever I want to." He followed her glance to his lunch and had no more to say.

The next day when Clara opened her lunch pail, a frog jumped out of it. The children roared.

"All right," said Miss Crumb, "we'll stay indoors during recess until the guilty one confesses."

A chorus of protest went up but stopped as Miss Crumb stood and glared at them. After eating and putting their pails away, they sat in their seats waiting. Loud whispers were heard around the room from time to time.

"Jack," she heard a whisper, "You know you did it. Confess, so we can go outside!"

"No I didn't," another voice said.

"Miss Crumb, Jack did it."

"I said confess, not tattle," Miss Crumb reminded.

"Haw, I did it," Jack said. "You weren't fair yesterday, Miss Haff."

"Jack you sit there, and the rest of you go outside," Miss Crumb said.

The children happily filed outside in the cold for some exercise and fresh air. Jack sat in surprise at being kept inside.

"I'll tell my dad when I get home," he threatened.

"You go ahead, Mr. Hanes. You need a good thrashing. That's what your father will do to you."

They never heard any more from Jack about the subject, but Clara did pay a visit to Elma's house on Saturday.

Elma answered her knock and looked up with questioning eyes.

"Hello Elma, I'm here to visit your mother."

"She's sick and can't get out of bed," Elma said.

"Why don't you let me in to see if I can do anything for her?"

The little girl slyly opened the door and let her in. The small cabin was untidy and cold.

In the corner of a cold room was a bed with a woman in it. Clara could hardly see a hump above the disheveled covers.

Clara quickly added wood to the cook stove and straightened the bedding. The woman was pasty white, and her arms stuck out like bird's claws. "Where is your father?" Clara asked Elma.

"He left before Christmas, and then Mama lost her baby she was carrying in her stomach."

Clara searched for some nourishment and found a dried-up potato. She made a soup of sorts for Elma and her mother. Going to the bed, she lifted the woman's head and spoon-fed her some of it. She was terribly dehydrated.

For the next few weeks Clara spent her money and time getting the house in order and baking every Saturday for them.

Anne, Elma's mother gained strength and encouragement from Clara.

Her husband had left to search for a job and found none. He returned to his family in early February a very defeated man.

One night at supper Clara asked Mr. Scott if he knew of a job for Anne's husband.

"Well, let me think. Maybe old Bob down at the coal yard could use some help. His rheumatism is giving him fits in this cold weather. I'll go talk it over with him tomorrow."

So it was arranged for Anne's husband, Jim, to work with "old Bob".

Anne and Clara became good friends.

The two woman sat having tea one afternoon. "Clara, I sense a melancholy in you. What has happened?" Anne asked.

Clara explained the story to her. Anne searched Clara's face and said, "I remember when I wanted to marry a young man. Mama and Daddy wouldn't let me. I moped around the whole winter, and in spring they sent me off, bag and baggage, to live with an aunt. What a horrible experience that was. My aunt was bitter because she had lost someone she loved, and she never married. She became so bitter about it that she took it out on anyone who would listen. I was her captive audience. When I was finally allowed to come home, the love of my life had left town. Then, when I had had time to mature, Jim came into my life, a good Christian man, and I found out what love truly was. He would do anything for me. He's really a very responsible man and will do anything to support us—that's honest. His love for God is great, and I am so happy in our Christian relationship. I heard my friend, whom I thought I was in love with, landed in prison for fraud. How close I came! But I do know what you are going through now, and I understand. Talk to me anytime." They both had suffered loss. Anne, the loss of her baby, and Clara, so many losses, made them able they were able to empathize with each other.

"Oh, thank you for sharing that. It really does help," Clara said.

Clara was taken to Battle Creek to meet her sister Rosemond during spring break.

She stayed at Aunt Rilla's house with them. The two sisters spent many happy hours together seeing the town. Clara liked Battle Creek very much.

"Oh, wouldn't it be nice if you could get a teaching position over here?" Rosemond asked.

"Well I can try. I really want us to be closer. Sister is such a special relationship."

All too soon the week was over, and Clara was taken back. She was overjoyed to be back in school with those children, who she now realized had become so precious to her.

She watched the progress of learning and the lights go on as they caught on to an idea.

Spring bloomed as only spring in Michigan can, with new life all around and the smells of spring and brooks gurgling after spring rains that washed everything clean.

Clara realized, along with the earth being restored, that her heart had been restored also. Oh, she still missed Morris, but she was beginning to realize life would go on, and God had plans for her life. *I will start praying for a Christian husband*, she thought. Whatever his plans were, she knew they would be good, for God is good.

Chapter 35

AFTER THE SEMESTER ENDED, Clara went back to Kalamazoo, after reluctantly saying goodbye to her friends in Richland.

It was finally time for graduation. Clara went to the train station to meet her family, Finally the train pulled in into Kalamazoo. Her father and brothers stepped off, and when Father saw her he swung her off her feet in a hug. "Oh, it's so good to see all of you again," she said when he put her down. "It feels like a lifetime since I saw any of you."

Her brothers all had hugs and kisses for her, too. Stowing their baggage in a locker, they all trooped downtown to book a room and eat at the local hotel in town. They had a lot of catching up to do.

Arriving at the hotel they sat down and ordered tempting sounding pot roast, the special of the day. While they waited to be served, they started chatting.

"Clara you look wonderful! That country air did you some good," Father said. "it works every time."

"Clara, I joined the Navy," said Forest.

"Oh, that's out of the blue!"

"I want to see the world, and I can't think of a better way. Those big battle ships have always intrigued me."

"Well we're in peacetime now, so let's just hope it stays that way."

"Well, after the World War, I think people have learned their lesson. I'll be leaving for boot camp in two weeks."

"Then I'm so glad I got this chance to see you. How is school going, Francis? Are you still settled on the ministry?"

"Yes, more than ever. However I did meet someone special. I think she will complete the picture for me, and we will serve the Lord together."

"Oh, tell me about her."

"Well, her name is Frances too, only spelled differently. I think that's what made us notice each other. She comes from a Nazarene family."

"Clara," said Walter, not wanting to be outdone, "Father and I have finally cleared the land and planned all the acreage."

"Well, it took this strapping young man to do it," said Father.

So the conversation went on. The food was delivered and enjoyed, and then it was time to call it a night. Tomorrow was a big day.

Waking early the next morning, Clara opened her eyes and was startled by her surroundings. The rosebud wallpaper, dark furniture and organdy ruffled curtains were still the same. Looking around, she came fully awake and realized where she was. She became excited and jumping out of bed, went to the window and looked out. The same garden and bench greeted her. A squirrel looked at her from a tree branch like he recognized her. It was so good to be back in Mrs. Doolittle's boarding house. Of course, she noticed Morris' absence everywhere. She looked down at the bench again. *That's where we first became acquainted*, she thought. How poignant her senses became. *But I'm a different person now. Because of my experiences in Richland, I can look forward to the future again. I know God has plans for me. My life is in front of me. Anything is possible. He will take care of me and give me an abundant life. That's one thing I've learned.*

She sat down and wrote Orpha a long letter, telling her of her conclusions she had reached and the peace and elation she was experiencing.

Clara's Father, Francis, Walter, and Forest were coming for breakfast at the boardinghouse. They had stayed at a hotel in town and would see her graduate.

She bathed and brushed and combed her long auburn hair until it shone. Knotting coils around her head and over her ears, she checked the effect in the mirror over her dresser. Her cheeks were blushed pink, and her eyes were glowing. *Not bad at all*, she thought.

Dressing in her starched and ironed white ruffled blouse, compliments of Mrs. Doolittle, she slipped her blue serge shirt over her head.

She hurried down to answer the bell, and was greeted by her spiffy father and brothers.

They hugged and kissed and compliments flew all around.

"Katura, (her father's pet name for her from childhood) I have never seen you look better. I am busting at my seams!" The mood was light and jovial.

Breakfast was a happy and talkative affair, and then they hurried off to school for the ceremonies.

The Dean of the school spoke at the commencement. The year was 1927. The country had been through a war, and times now seemed good. Progress was the wave of the future. People were optimistic.

Clara slipped on her robe, and the class was ushered onto the lawn in front of the school. People were sitting in chairs and standing or sitting on the lawn. Blue skies were overhead, and bright green trees dotted the landscape. The grass was newly cut. A platform had been erected for the graduating class. Her professors were seated in their respective garb, looking very official.

Clara glanced back to see her father and brothers beaming. They had managed to get chairs near the front. She caught Francis' eye, and he gave her a nod of approval and a big smile.

The ceremony began. First came a line of dignitaries, and then finally the graduating class was called, one at a time, to walk across the platform and be presented with their diplomas.

Finally it was Clara's turn. She felt weak in the knees at first. Then Mama and the heavens seemed to be looking down and smiling. *Good going!* They seemed to say. She walked on air across the stage and was handed her diploma. She was graduating with honors. What a proud moment!

From the audience her father whooped and hugged her brothers. "She made it! That little strap of a girl made it!"

She looked in the back of the crowd to see Morris watching her. He smiled and held up his thumb to her. Her heart stopped a moment before the next beat. Afterward, she had a chance to talk to him. "Is there any chance you will change your mind and marry me?" he asked.

"Not unless you've decided to follow the Lord." Clara looked up at him hopefully.

"No, I can't do that. I would be a hypocrite. I can see that you're happy. I will leave now. I really want you to find someone who shares your faith."

"I know God has plans for my life, and I'm looking forward to the future he has for me," Clara said to Morris. With that, she turned back to her family and her future.

Epilogue

M Y MOTHER, CLARA HAFF, did indeed move to Battle Creek, Michigan. She took a job the summer after graduation at Post cereals, and stayed once again at a boardinghouse, which was operated by Mr. and Mrs. Edgar Hamilton, who also had an adopted daughter, Bernice. Josie Hamilton was afflicted with cancer and eventually died.

After a period of time, Edgar and Clara fell in love and married.

It was a May – December marriage, my father having lost his first wife in his early twenties, married Josie, and when she died, he married Clara, thirty years younger but the love of his life.

They were married twenty-seven years and had four children-- Paul Edgar, Lois Christine, (my mother never forgot the baby sister she named Lois and lost.) My middle name Christine was after her great grandfather Peter Christian Jensen who came to this country from Denmark as a young man, Peters' daughter, and my mother's grandmother names were Christine), Wilfred James, and my baby sister, Joann Marie. Clara's father died when she was pregnant with me. She and my Aunt Rosemond were always close, and we shared holidays with her family of four girls every year as we grew up.

Things were not always easy for my mother. She had my brother Paul, then three years later me, then Will two and one half years later, and my sister sixteen months after that. Paul and I both contracted scarlet fever when I was in the first grade. My mother came down with it after that. Mother's case was the worst and left her in a weakened condition. Therefore it was difficult to raise four feisty children.

I lost my father when I was 26 years old. My mother was 54. Never having worked outside her home since her marriage, she learned how to drive and took a job as a cashier at a local hospital in the cafeteria.

She never lost her drive for education. She was an inspiration to each of us children. We all loved her, and her Christian example brought us to a saving knowledge of Christ.

When my husband Vern had open-heart surgery at age 53, my mother came and stayed with me. My husband's life was in danger, and on an hour-long ride home with her, she told me, "When Daddy died, I lay down on the bed, and I wanted to die too, but I've done an awful lot of living since then." She had too!

My parents were both storytellers. We children would sit on the floor in the evenings and listen to all the stories of their childhoods and traditions carried down through the generations.

I cherished these stories in my heart and turned out to be a storyteller, too. I can see this trait in some of my children and grandchildren also.

My mother Clara died at age 89, having lived a full life. She was always interested in what was going on around her. We could all see those snappy hazel eyes watch with interest. She was loved by all who knew her.

Printed in the United States
By Bookmasters